lov**e your**
library

Buckinghamshire Libraries
0845 230 3232
www.buckscc.gov.uk/libraries

24 hour renewal line
0303 123 0035

D0810035

For Richard Barlow

Apart from some close family members and memories, this is a work of fiction. Other names, characters, places, and incidents are either the product of the author's imagination or, if real, are used fictitiously.

The book is set in the late 1960s, though its themes are still relevant to the present day.

338 Euston Road, London NW1 3BH
Orchard Books Australia
Level 17/207 Kent Street, Sydney, NSW 2000

First published in the UK in 2011 by Orchard Books

ISBN 978 1 40831 302 2

Text © Vincent Caldey 2011

The right of Vincent Caldey to be identified as the author of this work
has been asserted by him in accordance with the Copyright,
Designs and Patents Act, 1988.

A CIP catalogue record for this book is available from the British Library.

1 3 5 7 9 10 8 6 4 2

Printed in Great Britain

Orchard Books is a division of Hachette Children's Books,
an Hachette UK company.

www.hachette.co.uk

VINCENT CALDEY

ORCHARD

BUCKS COUNTY LIBRARIES	
066359594 Y	
PET	
	29-Jul-2011
£5.99	IVH

PART ONE
before Prestonne

ONE

There's this blond-haired boy I see in the mornings. He goes to the school down at my end of town. The old-fashioned building. The posh place. The Grammar. Me, I go to Chevington, at his end of town.

So this is how it is: every morning we pass. He goes to one school, I go to the other. So maybe you're thinking I look for him coming? But I keep my head down. I don't pull faces. I concentrate my gaze on the cracks in the pavement. I don't want to see this boy.

But he sees me.

Somewhere near the butcher's. Or Wheeler's Garage. Or the boarded-over place all stuck with posters. I can always tell he's coming by the clip of his shoes.

"You," he says.

He bangs a hand through my shoulder. Spins me off balance. Into the shop fronts.

"What?" I say. But I know the answer.

"What?" he says. "What? You *what*?"

"Nothing," I say.

"Whadd'ya mean, *nothing*?"

I take a sideways step. He takes a bigger step. I step the other way. We dance on the pavement. The two boys with him, they snort at the sky. One of them lights up a fag for the other.

"Please," I say.

"*Please*," he says back.

"I'll be late for school."

"What do I care?" he says. He smells of tobacco, cold stale beer.

Sometimes, I get to taste this on his spit.

But on the day it all happened, the day it really kicked off, that was the day he got too rough. He'd been at me before, in all sorts of ways. A pinch of the cheeks. Tweak of the nipple. The worst he'd ever done was the thing with the lighter. Held me by the throat and pushed my head against a wall, spread my legs and watched me squirm.

I could smell my pants charring before he'd let me go.

But on this day, he has a new toy to play with.

"Do you like it?" he says. He shows me a knife.

Red. Swiss Army. Second-hand. Scratched. It has a corkscrew. A file. A tiny pair of scissors. Every instrument of torture. There, in his fist.

"Do you *like* it?" he says. He snarls like a bear.

"I love it," says his mate.

"Shut up," says the boy. He glares at me hard. Pale blue eyes. Cold. Unforgettable.

"Please," I say.

He puts a knee into my groin. I want to look away, but I daren't miss a trick.

His pretty mouth curls up, the same way as his hair. I hear a kind of click. Something glints below my eye. "Not gonna ask you again," he says.

"Cut him," says his mate.

"Shut *up*," says the boy. Slowly, he touches the blade to my face. He slides it flat along the side of my nose. "Do you like it?" he says, in a whisper this time.

I don't, but I nod. I have to agree. I just do what he says. To live. To get away.

"It's sharp," he says.

And almost wet against my skin. A tear leaves my eye. Pee trickles down my leg.

"Don't cry," he says. He sounds disappointed. But how can I be brave with a blade at my eye?

Then he grabs my shirt, low down by the flaps. He

stretches it tight and he slashes the knife. I hardly hear the rip as he takes a pace back. He looks down at his work and runs a thumb along the blade. "Neat," he says and throws me a wink. He folds the knife away and drops it in his pocket. He backs off, pointing a finger at my head. "I'll see you around," he says.

TWO

You see how it is? The corner I'm in? You understand now why I don't talk at breakfast? Why I push my porridge round the bottom of my dish and my grandfather gets at me to sit up straight? Buses pass. That's what I want to tell him. Buses pass. They never stand and talk. I want to beat the table till the crockery dances. If they'd put me on a bus to school, I wouldn't be like this.

But they don't. So I stir. Round and round goes the porridge. Till it's cold. Till even Ginger, the dog, won't have it. And my ear takes a clipping from my grandfather's palm. And my grandmother says to him, "Ease off, Len. The boy…" She doesn't finish. She doesn't want to say. That's the conversation that leads to my mother.

And nobody wants to talk about my mother.

My grandfather straightens the knot of his tie. He runs a hand of brittle bones across his shining forehead. His slicked hair looks like the surface of a melon, his skin the texture of a sagging leather ball. "There's no excuse for slovenly behaviour," he says. He leans in, smelling of something called formalin. A product of his work with the dead, Nana says. He wags a crooked finger. His cufflink is undone. "Smarten up," he says to me. "And don't be late for school."

THREE

On days like this, I always think about Stevie. About the estate. How I got into this fix. How I came to be living in my grandparents' house, going to the school at the other end of town.

We were just two kids. Four houses apart. Two mop-haired boys. Being mates. Having fun. Catching sticklebacks together in Overdale Brook. Playing footie on the rec. Getting dirt on our knees.

One day, the day it all started to slide, I was going back to Stevie's house for tea. Number 20. Stone-cladding. Bike in the garden. Blue Cortina jacked up on the drive. We went round the back like we always did. Crept to the door so we wouldn't wake his sister. Little baby Cheryl, sleeping out the afternoon. Through the kitchen window, we saw Stevie's mum. Sitting on a worktop. Kissing a man. Her legs were wrapped around him, crossed behind his bum.

Stevie went in. He said, "Mum, what you doin'?"

They both said, "Shit!" Stevie's mum and the man. Ryan Benedict it was. He fixed cars in the garage off Wetherby Road. There was oil on his cheek, a rag in his pocket, a patch of scarlet lipstick in the shadows of his throat.

"I thought you were out, you little…" Stevie's mum clenched her teeth and caught a nervous breath. She pulled the arm of her blouse back onto her shoulder. I saw a flash of white cotton as she slid off the worktop. "What do you think you're looking at?" she said.

Ryan Benedict turned. Cocksure. Mean. His sideburns bristled on his upturned collar. He spat a piece of chewing gum into the sink. His head was nod nod nod nod nodding, like the dogs you see in the backs of cars. From the side of his mouth he said, "Deal with Stevie." His oil-black eyes came down on me.

Stevie's mum yanked Stevie into the front.

I was still holding the stickleback jar.

Ryan Benedict nodded at the sink. 'Put the jar down on the drainer,' he was saying. I was scared. The jar wobbled and crashed into the sink.

"Leave it," he said, as I scrabbled among the pots.

But the sticklebacks?

"*Leave it*." He whacked me. Hard. I slammed

against the back door, cracking the glass. The key fell out. The star-shaped flowers on the table dropped a petal. Upstairs, baby Cheryl began to cry.

Ryan Benedict said to me, "What did you see?"

I clutched my shoulder and looked at the sink.

"Oi?!" he said. He put two fingers like a gun to my head.

"You and Stevie's mum were kissing," I said.

"No, we weren't," said Ryan. "What did you see?"

He twisted his fingers. Screwed the barrel. He smelled of aftershave, grease and oil. His fingernails were mixing it into my blood.

In the front, I heard Stevie's mum call out, "You tell no one, got it? *No one* – or you're dead."

Eyes tight shut, I said, "I didn't see nothing."

"Yeah, you did," said Ryan, hissing like a snake. "You saw me outside, changing a wheel. On the drive. Gettin' dirty. I was never in the kitchen. Might have had a cuppa. On the drive. Okay?"

"Okay," I said.

"Where was I?"

"On the drive."

His fingers pushed my head down, level with my shoulder. "Positive?"

"Yeah."

He stepped away. "Good." He cracked his knuckles. "Good," he said again, and slapped my ear. Just hard enough to let me know how much he could hurt me. "Now, get out of my way. I've got work to do, you prick."

He bundled me aside and opened the door.

Stevie's mum burst in crying, "Ryan! Ryan!" The veins of her eyes were shot with blood. "Ryan?" she screamed. But he was already gone. She slammed the door, making it bounce against the frame. As she turned, she almost looked surprised to see me. "Why don't you just piss off home, you creep?"

I saw Stevie in the next room, covering his eye. I walked to the sink, not looking at his mother. I picked up my jam jar and drained the last dregs on the washing-up pile. The plates were stuck with egg yolk, sauce and beans. There was an upturned fly on the window sill. A pregnant drip from the crusted tap. Around the plug hole, tea leaves told their own story. I looked for my fish and saw a stickleback squirming in the prongs of a fork. One stickleback that should have stayed in Overdale Brook. It suffocated right there in front of my eyes.

Lately, I've been wondering how that stickleback felt.

FOUR

My grandmother got to know something was up. She wanted the story on the rip in my shirt. "How did you get this, here?" she said.

"What?" I said, looking. "It's nothing. A tear." I was reading a comic. I didn't want to talk. I didn't want to think about the blond-haired boy. I balanced my feet on Ginger's body. His doggy hairs tickled through the holes in my socks. He made a whining noise and clawed at the rug.

"You'll have to use the other shirt tomorrow," she said. She was sitting in the rocking chair, threading a needle, looking through the eye of the needle at me.

She needed an explanation, I knew. She was using small talk to squeeze the truth out. I read. She talked small. Some stuff about the hole. The size of it. The edge. Clean, was what she said. The edge was clean.

So I made up a story. I made up a lie. "We were running in the yard and I fell, that's all. I ripped it on the gravel. I was meaning to tell you."

She tugged a line of cotton from the flaps of the shirt. "No," she said, "you didn't do that."

The pages of the comic fluttered in my hands.

"Gravel doesn't cut like this," she said.

"I was *running*," I said, but my voice had gone.

In the budgie cage, Willoughby left his perch. My grandmother said what a pretty boy he was.

The line of his mouth. The sweep of his hair. Oh, what a pretty boy he was.

"Who were you running from?" she said.

I looked away, acid drops forming in my eyes.

My grandmother moved the shirt off her lap. She came and sat on the sofa beside me. "Tell me," she said. She pushed my fringe aside.

And I let it all out about the blond-haired boy.

FIVE

I was wiping back a tear when Uncle Billy walked in.
"What's this? What's the matter with him?" he said.

Nana looked up. "Some boy on the street. A bully
from the Grammar." She stroked my arm.

Uncle Billy came over and held me by the chin. He
twisted my face up into the light. "Where?" he said.
"Where's he been hit?"

My grandmother said, "This boy doesn't hit." She
showed him the line of stitches in my shirt.

My uncle nodded. He let go of my face. "How long
has this been going on?"

Weeks, I told him. Stretching into months.

"He's older," Nana said. "Stops him every day.
Along Berry Road, on the way to school."

From the doorway to the hall someone gave a light
cough. Graeme, my grandfather's new hired help, was

jingling coins in his overcoat pockets. "So take the guy down and nail him," he said, in a voice like a whisper from another world.

Uncle Billy said, "This is family, Graeme."

Graeme just smiled and took off his gloves. He called the dog to him and walked out without a word.

Uncle Billy opened up the mantelpiece clock. He drilled the key tightly, restoring the tick. "We need to deal with this," he said. "This has to be stopped."

My grandmother said, "His father is the one who should deal with it, Billy."

"His father drives lorries," my Uncle Billy said.

Dad would be away for another two days, delivering shoes to shops in the north.

Uncle Billy walked back to me and picked up a cushion. He plumped it into shape with the side of his fist. "This has to be stopped," he said again, to me. He arranged the cushion in the corner of the sofa. "Okay, this is what we're going to do."

SIX

It wasn't me who grassed up Ryan Benedict.

We all heard the rumpus. The whole estate. Like a spark going off in a fireworks box. At 20 Meadowcliffe, stuff began to fly. Crockery. Furniture. Anger. Words.

He called her a slag. He called her a tart.

He was useless, she yelled back.

It all went off.

People gathered. They buzzed like flies. They muttered about the kids. Shouldn't someone call the cops?

Mrs Allenby from 26 shook her head. She had her hair in a scarf and a fag on her lip. "Like an accident waiting to happen," she said. She tapped some ash onto Stevie's lawn.

Mrs Bannerjee said, "But what about the children?"

The window of an upstairs room flew back. Out came a suitcase, clean through the gap. The parachute opened on Stevie's mother's life. Her underwear spilled into the Sunday morning. Knickers and bras the colour of tinsel. Stockings and suspenders. Satin and lace. All of it landed in the cold grey drizzle.

"He'll kill her. He's got previous," someone said.

Shoes, like clay pigeons, sailed across the lawn.

Mrs Allenby lifted her toe.

"There is a *baby* in there," Mrs Bannerjee said, knocking her small brown fists together.

A horn went *pap!* in the middle of the road. A guy in a turban and a frilly purple shirt stepped out of an unwashed taxi cab.

"What's happening?" he said, with a jut of his chin.

"What isn't?" someone said.

Stevie's mum let out a wail.

Mr Jewson from next door said, "He's slapped her."

The taxi driver chewed a mound of gum. It clung to his teeth like melted cheese. He pushed through the crowd and rapped the door. "Hey, hey! Taxi!" He drilled the bell.

In the house, Stevie's dad began to shout. "Is it mine? Is it? Is it, you tart?"

"I'm leaving! Just stay away from me, right?"

"Answer me, you cow. *Is it mine?*"

There was a bang. Loud. A real heart shaker.

Stevie's mother screamed.

I heard Stevie shout, "No!"

A baby carrier landed on the lawn, face down.

"Jesus," said the cabbie. His chewing stopped. Everything stopped.

And everybody stared.

Mrs Bannerjee fumbled the carrier over. "Empty," she said. She fell to her knees and clamped her hands in prayer.

"Someone put the suitcase in the car," said the cabbie. He pushed back his sleeves and flicked away his gum. "You. Come on." He beckoned Mr Jewson.

One… Two… They shouldered the door.

There was shouting. Threats. Some kind of a struggle. The cabbie said, "It's just a fare, man. A fare."

Stevie's mother staggered out like a newborn calf. One heel broken. Blood on her lip. She was clutching baby Cheryl tight to her breast. Stevie was in his red football kit, looking back bewildered as she dragged him up the path. He was reaching out behind him as far as he could stretch, but the paper chain back to his dad was cut.

His dad filled the doorway, playing Samson. Black

hairs weaving through the strings of his vest. He said, "Tracey, baby. Tracey, don't go." But he didn't try to stop her. He didn't step out. He just hung in the frame like a spider's web.

A screech of tyres took the taxi away.

And my head wasn't sure but my heart was certain that I'd never see Stevie again after that. And all I could think as I walked up the road was: 'I'm glad this isn't happening to my mum and dad...'

SEVEN

It was the weekend. No school. It was all to our advantage. We had time to work it out, my Uncle Billy said. He wouldn't tell me anything more right then. But that Sunday, after lunch, he took me outside. He stood me on the drive of my grandfather's business, between the narrow coffin store and the chapel of rest. He said to me, "Pick up a piece of gravel. Close your hand round it. Tell me what you feel."

I could feel a piece of gravel in the centre of my palm.

He nodded. "Close your hand tighter," he said.

I felt the stone biting at the layers of my skin.

"Again," he said. "*Tighter*. Tell me what you feel."

Blood trickling from the centre of my palm.

"Good." He blew a little air through his nose. He pursed his lips. He looked satisfied now. "That's as tight as your fist needs to be tomorrow morning – when you hit this boy."

"*What?*" I said.

"When he starts up next time, you stand back, you swing. You don't talk to him or give him any kind of warning. You just aim for his chin and you hit him. Hard. We'll give that bully what bullies deserve. Turn him whiter than the stiffs, okay?"

He was talking about the bodies in the fridge next door.

"But he'll beat me," I said. "He'll beat me flat."

My Uncle Billy smiled. He rubbed his palms. He threw gravel at the crows on the roof of the chapel. I was his brother's son, he said. He told me everything was going to be all right. He had that look in his eye, the look I've seen before when they gave him medals. Uncle Billy has medals for outdoor survival. He rescues people from mountains sometimes.

Tyres splashed a puddle at the front of the drive. Ginger started yapping and ran to see. Graeme pulled up in the long hearse, Betty. We have names for all our funeral cars: Betty, Alice, Mary Lou.

"That's why you're gonna be all right," said Billy.

I looked at Graeme as he stepped out of the car. He blew warm air into the cup of his hands. He put out a fist for Ginger to sniff, then punched the dog's nose when he got too close.

"Graeme's coming?"

"Not Graeme, the car."

Betty? How would Betty make me safe?

Uncle Billy read my face. "You walk. I drive."

"You're gonna follow me?" I said. "You're gonna follow me in the car?"

Uncle Billy stared out across the Lancashire plain. "All you have to do is the hitting," he said.

EIGHT

Later, by the coffin store, Graeme called me in. He was
in his brown work coat. Knee-length. Clean. The one
that makes him look like a woodwork teacher. He was
working overtime, lining a coffin. Prettying a box with
cream satin trim.

I rolled against the doorway, Ginger at my side. I've
always liked the coffin store. It doesn't freak me out. It
has what Nana calls 'a masculine smell'. Oak and resin.
Fresh new wood. Sawdust patterning the terracotta
floor.

Graeme had the arc lamp pulled down low. It was
picking up the varnish of the empty boxes, filling up
the room with an amber glow. "So, you gonna paste this
guy tomorrow?"

"Did Uncle Billy tell you what we're going to do?"

Graeme said, "Yep. Shall I wash the hearse?"

"Funny," I said. But I took his point. I looked around the store at the stacks of coffins. Maybe tomorrow, one would have my name on it.

Graeme cracked the handle on a staple gun. A staple landed in the weave of my sweater. "Me and you, kiddo, we need to get along."

Kiddo. I hate it when he calls me that. "Why?" I said. It was a reasonable question. Graeme only works here. He lifts and shifts. I don't have to get along with him. I don't even have to talk to him. Now and then we knock a ball round the yard together. When he can be bothered. When Grandad's not about.

He lobbed the staple gun into the coffin. "Billy's going climbing. Six-week course. And I need somewhere to crash for a while."

Rowf, barked Ginger, as if he knew.

But I never knew. "You're moving in?"

"Shame not to keep the sheets warm," he said.

"Nana never said anything to me."

"So?"

"It's just…"

"What? You calling me a liar?" He picked up a hammer and rolled it in his fist.

I shook my head. I didn't know what to say. For a moment, I was staring at cracks in the pavement.

"Come here," he said, but I could only gulp. He smirked and put the hammer into place on the rack. "Here," he said again, pointing out a spot. His voice sucked me in like a cold November fog. "Let me teach you something cool – about fighting. Your blond-haired kid, he's playing a game. This thing on the street. This jolly with the knife. He didn't stick you in the shirt tails, he stuck you in the head. He wasn't going to cut you. He hasn't got the balls. If he'd waved a frigging lollipop under your nose the result would have been exactly the same. Doesn't matter what kind of weapon he has. It's not about what he intends to do. It's about what he makes you *think* he might do." His gaze drifted over the racks of tools. Screwdrivers. Drills. A whole row of chisels.

Was he saying I should take one with me tomorrow?

A moth got dizzy around the lamp. In a flash, Graeme snatched it up, mid-flight. With his free hand he loosened the buttons of his coat. "If you want to hurt your bully boy, this is where you hit him." He pressed one finger to the side of his head. There was a spider web caught in his tight, permed hair. "Here," he said again, tapping his temple. "Where the fear breeds. Where the pain lasts." He stared at his closed fist. "Dead or alive?"

Dead. Had to be. Crushed to a pulp.

He blew on his fingers. *Ali-kazam*. When he opened his hand, the moth fluttered free.

My heartbeat flew around the boxes with it.

He saw my eyes growing huge and he smirked again. "Make him believe you've got magic in your fist and he'll never come near you again. Got it?"

He tugged at the light pull. The store turned black. Twilight bathed one half of the coffins. "You're gonna be a hero tomorrow," he said, as if he knew more than he was letting on. I saw a crown glinting on the arc of his teeth. He gathered up the silence and patted my cheek. "I'll take the bed by the window," he said.

NINE

I told my mother what I'd seen at Stevie's. "His mum left. His dad hit her. We thought he'd killed the baby. She took Stevie in a taxi. Will they come back?"

She was standing at the sink by the kitchen window. Looking at the garden. Drying pots. Quietly she said, "It's none of our business."

"But what about Stevie?"

"You've got other friends," she said.

Some. Not many. None as good as him. "She had to drag him," I said. "He didn't want to go."

She pushed her tea towel slowly round a plate. "A child needs to be with its mother," she said.

"He didn't want to go," I told her again.

She put the plate down and picked up a cup.

I asked her, "Mum, when's Dad coming home?"

"Wednesday."

Oh. "Is he staying at Nana's?"

She parted the blinds, made an eye onto the world. Her gaze went deep into the garden again. "That's what he says."

"Why didn't he take me with him?" At half term, I normally get a ride in the van.

"You have to see the dentist tomorrow," she said.

Mouthwash, drills and a numb gob. Great. "When are we going to Nana's again?"

"We don't have the money for holidays," she said.

I said, "It's just Nana's. It's not a *proper* holiday." Not like Skegness. Caravans. The beach. But I like it all the same. I'm happy at Nana's. The house is big and strange and old. The staircase creaks like the knees of a giant. Coal crackles in the ash-scarred grate. From the garden, if you look across the Lancashire plain, Blackpool Tower sits up on the horizon. Blackpool Tower, the size of a matchstick. Sometimes I wave at the tourists there and wonder if they're waving back at me. Then there's Ginger, digging up Grandad's potatoes. Ginger, the best friend a boy could ever have. Dad has always promised me we're going to have a dog.

A dog would be cool.

Now Stevie's gone.

Mum sighed and put the cup down on the rack. She

wasn't in the mood to talk about dogs. "I want to ask you something," she said.

I looked around the kitchen. It was just me and her. Charmaine and Beverley were playing on the swing. I could hear their voices out in the garden. "What?" I said. She sounded serious.

She folded the tea towel, took a deep breath. "If me and your father ever split up, who would you want to be with the most?"

Split up? Mum and Dad? After what I'd just seen? I felt as if the air had been sucked from my chest. I picked up a fork and scratched at the table, carving lines in the blue Formica.

"Stop that," she said. She turned round slowly. "I've told you before not to mark the table." I couldn't see her well against the kitchen window, just a cascade of thick brown hair. "Tell me," she said, "who would it be?"

In a whisper I told her, "I'd go with you." I thought it was what she wanted to hear. A child needs to be with its mother, right?

She came to the table and took my hand. Hers were still warm from the washing-up water. "I love you," she said. "Will you do something for me?"

Her eyes were so brown, like deep red conkers.

"I've been invited out," she said. "Some people from work are having a party. If I go, do you think you can sit for the girls?"

She was rubbing my hand now, waiting for a genie.

"Why did you ask who I'd go with?" I said.

Her gaze dipped, as if she was searching for something, something she might have lost long ago. "It's nothing. I was just musing," she said.

I thought about Stevie's dad at the door. *Tracey, baby. Tracey, don't go.* "Don't you love Dad any more?" I said.

She drew my hand to her mouth and kissed it. Her lips felt soft and dry against my skin. "I will always love your father," she said. "Now, will you sit with the girls or not? I won't be out long. I'll give you some sweets. Bonbons. Your favourite. A bag to yourself. You'll have the telly. And your music. And your games. And the sweets."

"What if Charmaine starts crying?" I said. She's six. She has dreams about bogeymen and monsters.

Mum backed away, twiddling her wedding ring. "If there's any kind of trouble you can fetch Mrs Allenby."

Mrs Allenby? 'Fag ash Lil' we called her. I didn't want that grumpy old bag in our house, poking her nose into our affairs. She had laughed when Stevie's mum drove off. "What's an accident waiting to happen?" I said.

Mum frowned. She seemed thrown. But I knew she'd have an answer. She's clever. She does typing for people at the Council. "It's what people say when something's unavoidable."

Stevie's mum and dad. Breaking up. Unavoidable.

The door rattled open. Charmaine ran in. "Mummy, Beverley fell off the swing." She plonked a shoe on the table, then she was gone.

Mum sighed. She hooked her apron on the back of the door. She paused a moment, tightening her lip. "Tonight," she said. "I'll be going out tonight."

Then she picked up the shoe and went into the garden.

T E N

So I walked to school on the Monday morning. I didn't have a satchel. My arms were swinging free. I had to get a really good swing at this boy. That's what my Uncle Billy had said. Uncle Billy took care of the little things, the satchel. All I carried was the gravel in my palm.

At Wheeler's, I saw the blond boy coming. He nudged his friend and nodded me out. Wide, square shoulders. Shortish. Stocky. Crisp black jacket. Steel-capped shoes. The blue and yellow tie of Prestonne Grammar. The hair, like surf, sweeping right across the forehead, hiding the eyes and the dangers there.

"You," he says, approaching. "You looking at me?"

This is the first time proper, yes. I didn't know before, he has a dimple in his chin. So that's where I hit him. In the dimple. In the chin. A punch that makes the gravel bite into my palm. The blond boy staggers. His bottom lip drops. His bottom lip judders and he can't close his mouth. His face changes colour: whiter than a stiff.

"Jesus, Frankie..." his one friend says. The lighted cigarette slips through his fingers.

I stand back, shaking. My knuckles feel raw. I stretch my fingers and drop the gravel. Blood is running from the centre of my palm.

Then a hearse pulls up beside Wheeler's Garage. A Ford Fairlaine that I know as Betty. Lines of silver trim running down her sides. She looks like a great black rocket ship.

Uncle Billy leaps out of the seat. "You," he says. Now it's all turned round. One stab of his finger pushes Frankie back. "You. That's right. I want your name."

Frankie stares at the car. He says his name: Lennox. Francis Lennox. What's this about?

Uncle Billy leans towards him, hands on his hips. "Don't try it on with me," he says. "You think this is clever? You think it's smart? Picking on a lad much younger than yourself?"

Frankie opens his mouth, but he's just sucking air.

"We never went near him," the other boy says.

"Shut up," says Billy. "I'm talking to him." He looks

Frankie Lennox in the eye once more. "Mr Gifford knows what you've been doing."

And it's like a guillotine has just come down.

Frankie sways as if he's going to be sick.

Uncle Billy snaps his fingers and brings him to attention. "Right. Here's what you're going to do. When you get to school, you're going to report. You don't hang around swapping notes with your mates. No crafty fags behind the bike sheds first. You go straight in and you speak to Mr Gifford. He'll be waiting for you. Mr Gifford. Are we clear?"

Frankie nods. His eyes are swimming. He's not quite there. But his face says he knows Mr Gifford all right. Somewhere behind the pale blue eyes there is punishment worse than a punch to come.

"You know Compton Street?"

Frankie gives a nod.

"From now on, that's your route to school."

"What? That'll take us forever," says his mate. "I'd have to get up at seven for that."

"Then buy yourself a decent alarm clock," says Uncle Billy. "Now, get on your way. The pair of you. And don't ever touch this boy again."

And it's done. Frankie and his mate move off. All they leave behind are the cracks in the pavement and a strange uncomfortable shadow of fear.

We get into the hearse, Uncle Billy and me. He drives me to school in a funeral car. A slow, smooth ride all the way down the road. People nod. They take off their hats – even though we don't have a coffin in the back. Uncle Billy leans his elbow out of the window. "You did well back there. You left him pretty shaken. You should practice, though, on a bag or something."

"Practice?"

"You could have hit him harder," he says.

I don't know. I don't know about that. Suddenly, I've got this afterburn of nerves. Maybe I've punished Frankie enough. "Who's Mr Gifford? How do you know him?"

At the traffic lights for Greeley Road, we have to pull up. A chance for Uncle Billy to drum his fingers, to think about what he wants to say next. "I don't. Mr Gifford is a friend of Graeme's."

Graeme's? My heart skips a frightening beat. "How does Graeme know a teacher at the Grammar?"

Uncle Billy flicks the wipers. The screen clears of drizzle. A green light says we can roll again. "He was a caretaker at Prestonne before he came to us. Mr Gifford wrote Graeme his reference, I think. They still meet for a drink at the Cotton Arms in Hanford.

Graeme says they don't stand for bullying at Prestonne. He thought a tip-off to a teacher would help you out."

But I don't want Graeme helping me out. In some ways, he scares me more than Frankie. "You said this was family. We'll deal with it, you said."

Uncle Billy sighs and juts his chin. He loosens his black tie away from his throat. He works hard to be a proud and proper uncle, especially when his brother can't always be a dad. "When I leave next week he practically will be – family, I mean, fully paid up." He glances sideways, sees I've gone quiet. "He told me he told you he's moving in. It's only temporary, till he finds somewhere better."

He lets in the clutch just a shade too fast. The car lurches as he turns off Berry Road, swinging me against the passenger door. The smell of Betty's leather seats sickens me at times. But it's not the scent of leather that's bothering me now. I feel cheated. Nothing like a 'hero' at all. My one big punch was as hollow as the sky. The hole was dug for Frankie before I left the house. All he had to do was snap the twig. "I don't get it."

Uncle Billy shrugs as if he doesn't understand.

"If Mr Gifford already knew about Frankie, why did you make me go up and hit him?"

"You have to learn to stand up for yourself," he says. "Felt good, didn't it, getting even?"

No. I was scared. And the feeling hasn't gone. It's shifted to a dark and dangerous corner, but I can't quite see what the trouble is yet. "What will happen when Frankie reports?"

The car pulls up at the gates of the school. Uncle Billy jerks the handbrake as if he's necked a chicken. "He'll get some kind of warning, I suppose. He ought to thank Christ he's not in the mountains. I'd stuff him down a rabbit hole and leave him there. Go on, get yourself in to school. I'm helping your grandad with a funeral at ten."

I open the door and step out of the hearse, do the longer walk round the back of the car. My uncle hands me my satchel through the window.

"It's done," he says. "We sorted this out. When your dad gets home, we'll show him that punch." He winks at me proudly as Betty rolls away.

The bell rings, scattering pigeons off the roof. I hurry through a playground emptying of kids. I like school. I try hard. It's what my mother wants. But this morning it feels like I'm walking into prison. I'm halfway up the steps before I realise why. When Dad brought me here, to live in the north, my grandparents put me in the first school available: Chevington, a concrete secondary modern. But Nana's had her eye on a crisp black jacket, badge on the pocket, blue and yellow tie. I'm top of my class. Scholarship material. Next month I sit an entrance exam.

For Prestonne.

ELEVEN

On the Wednesday, my dad brought home a dog. An Alsatian. A puppy. A black and tan bundle. He put it down beside the fire and we all went crazy: me, Charmaine, Beverley...Mum.

"What the hell is that?" She sank into a chair with her hands in her lap.

My dad said, "Don't pull his ears, Charmaine. He might be small but he's got sharp teeth."

Bev said, "What shall we call him, Dad?"

"Bruce," said my dad, "his name is Bruce."

"Broo-ooce!" We shouted for him, under the sofa.

"Bruce?" said my mum. Her voice was level.

Dad winked at her and grinned. "Got it from a bloke I deliver to in Runcorn. He had six for sale. He—"

"You *bought* it?" Her head came up with a jerk.

"A present. For the kids."

"How much, Neville?"

"It's just money," he said. "We'll be all right."

"How much?" said my mum. There were tremors in her voice.

"I like to bring them something when I've been away," he said. He stepped up to cuddle her. She pushed him aside.

"We'll never stop paying for that," she said. "It'll cost more to feed than the damn kids will. And who's going to walk it?"

"I will," said Dad.

"When, Neville? You're never bloody here!"

"Don't swear in front of the kids," he said.

"And when we're at work? Who deals with it then?"

"We've got a garden. I'll make it a kennel to sleep in."

"Oh, will you?" she said. She yanked a tissue from her sleeve. "Well, make one for yourself as well while you're at it."

"What's that supposed to mean?" He tried to catch her arm.

But she was too quick. In the hall. Up the stairs. Sobbing.

"Marlene?" he shouted from the bottom of the stairs.

"If it's about the money, we've still got the loan your mother gave us."

A door slammed.

Silence.

He came back in.

"Daddy, Bruce has done a wet," said Charmaine.

I was standing in the middle of the room, looking on. Dad sighed and said to me, "Go and fetch a cloth."

I was heading for the kitchen when he clamped my shoulder. "What's this?" he said. He was pointing at my jumper. My spitfire banking through the wartime sky. There were cloudy white patches in the bright blue wool.

"Don't know," I said. I just lied, like I had to. I'd promised Mum I would, because that was the deal. When she gave me the bonbons, they came with a price: "Don't tell your father I'm going out. He'd be annoyed if he knew I'd left you to baby-sit."

And I'd stood at the window and watched her go, driven off by a man in a grey flannel suit, who opened car doors for her and smoked a cigar.

Icing sugar and bright blue wool.

The residue of bonbons.

The dust of guilt.

TWELVE

One dinnertime, Grandad called me to his office. He wanted to know what was happening at school.

"At school?" I said.

"I had a phone call," he said. He pointed at the phone as if he wanted me to guess. It sat on the corner of his leather-bound desk, next to a rose-coloured marble urn.

I squinted at the phone. It told me nothing.

"Mr Ireland is worried about your school work," he said.

I dropped my shoulders. I didn't want to know.

The office chair creaked. Grandad sat forward. He tapped his jotter with a fountain pen. "Stand up straight when I'm talking to you."

"I haven't done anything wrong," I said.

"You've been slacking," he said. "Not answering in

class. You've got exams next week. Your scholarship for Prestonne."

Prestonne. I felt my knees go weak. "I don't want to go to Prestonne," I said.

I hadn't seen Frankie since our fight at Wheeler's. But that hadn't stopped me thinking about him. It was like a dripping tap that I couldn't turn off. He knew all the corners. He knew all the tricks. He knew where the sun rose over the quad.

What would he do when he got me at Prestonne?

Drip.

Drip.

Drip.

Drip.

Grandad sighed. He took off his specs. He rubbed them on the worn-out lining of his jacket. "This is about that boy again, isn't it?"

"He'll kill me, Grandad. I don't want to go."

He pointed a finger, yellowed by tar. In the graveyard of his mouth, there were tombstones missing. "Stop whining and listen to me," he said. "You're not going to throw away a decent education just because of some barney on the street. That thug is not going to pick on you again. He's been threatened with expulsion, according to Graeme. He'll be out on his ear if he as much as breathes on another boy again. So forget this rubbish about not going to Prestonne and start to think about your family, for once. Get your head down and pass this exam. If you don't, then…"

"What?"

He pressed his thumbs into the arches of his eyes. He has migraines sometimes. Too much stress. Too much weight on his shoulders, Nana says. I know what she means: he carries more than coffins. He worries about his son, my dad.

"I wasn't going to tell you this," he said, "but in the circumstances, maybe you ought to know." He opened up his silver clip, took out a cigarette. He spoke with it jumping about on his lip. "Your dad's in trouble. He might go to prison."

"Prison?" I said, with a croak in my voice. "Why? Did he hit Philip again?"

His lighter flared. Smoke poured from his nose. "He's not been paying your mother enough maintenance. Not enough to satisfy the courts, at any rate. If he's jailed, she'll fight to take you away, to live with her and her boyfriend and the girls. She'll claim that your dad's not fit to look after you."

I shook my head. "I'm not going," I said.

He tipped some ash into the urn on the desk. "Then

be smart and get yourself sorted out at school. You win a place at Prestonne, it looks good for your dad."

And there it was, in smoke and whispers: swot myself into Frankie's lair, or leave Nana's house and live with my mother – and the man who took her away from my dad.

THIRTEEN

It was weeks, maybe months, before Dad knew – before I knew – what Mum was planning. It started with niggles. More slammed doors. Twisted arguments. The misery of love. When Bruce stole the Sunday joint off the cooker, I thought she might walk out there and then. But it didn't come then. It was slower, painful. The marriage wept like an open sore. Till it all fell apart like an old birds' nest, and the only thing left was the bonbon dust.

One night I met Philip, my mother's friend. I knew him now. He was a Friday night regular. Her smooth-haired boss. All pomp and smoke. Chauffeur. Escort. Calling card. Drawing ever closer like a wary fox. The garden gate. The doorstep. The chickens. He would straighten his tie before he rang the bell, leave fingerprints in hair gel on the push. The day he wiped his feet on the mat, it was done. He came in, soaking up the room through his specs: the telly, the sofa, the standard lamp, the three ducks flying up the chimney wall.

"Young man," he said to me. He crushed my hand. Soaked me up too, like a fixture and fitting. I could see through his lenses that I didn't matter. I was nothing. Her son. The first born.

Irrelevant.

That night, I fell asleep with Bruce on the rug. I remember how he growled when Philip picked me up. The telly was hissing, making snow. The air was full of gin and perfume and cigars. Philip carried me upstairs and took off my shoes. He put me into bed fully-clothed, full of dust. In the doorway, I saw my mother's silhouette. She was swaying, reaching for a shadow to dance with. They kissed in the closing light of the hall. My mother and Philip.

Philip and my mum.

In the morning, I woke to the clunk of a door. I was hot and sweating. I wanted to pee. But I stood at the window and looked down the street. The milkman was winking at Mrs Allenby, but she wasn't taking any notice of him. As she opened her purse to pay for her milk, she turned her head to look at a car, pulling slowly away from the house. She tucked her pint underneath her arm, sucked on her fag and stared at my window. The milkman came up and pinched her arse. Mrs Allenby called him a cheeky bugger. He jumped aboard his milk float and rattled up the road. Downstairs, somewhere, Bruce began to whine.

Mrs Allenby tipped some ash.

That weekend, Dad was a different man. No Jack the lad. No whistle. No swagger. No kites flying in his breezy sky. We took Bruce for a walk along the railway line. I was throwing sticks. For my dog. For the fun of it. Dad was punching the wells of his pockets. At the bridge, we stopped and looked back along the tracks.

Dad said, "I want to ask you something. Has anyone been to the house this week?"

I knew what he meant. I knew what he wanted. What I should have said. What he didn't want to hear. So I told him a half-truth, not quite a lie. "Mrs Bannerjee came on the borrow, three times."

"I don't mean Mrs Bannerjee," he said. He was squeezing his hands now, tight below his nose. He kept beating them slowly against his mouth. "Does your mum go out while I'm away, delivering?"

My eyes were on the railway, counting sleepers, watching them merge into a dull brown blur.

"Has she told you not to tell me?" he said.

In the distance, I saw the nose of a train. The wind drew a cold line around my ears. The rails began to sing. Bruce began to bark. The stone bridge shuddered. Trains flashed beneath us. Rattle and rock. Gruddle and pod. Mum and Dad. Going separate ways. Who should I stick with? Who should I betray?

In the settling quiet I said to my father, "I don't know."

Somewhere in the green fields a cockerel crowed.

And I knew there and then that the shame would never leave me.

My dad just nodded and turned up his collar. "Call Bruce. We're going home," he said.

FOURTEEN

The bed by the window was always Uncle Billy's. When Graeme took it over, I let him think he'd won.

"Stone me," he said. "Isn't this just the Hotel Grande?" He sat on the edge of the bed, looking round, smirking at Uncle Billy's posters of women. Film stars, mainly, or people off the telly. He pointed at Audrey Hepburn in *Tiffany's*, cocked a finger and blew her away.

He kicked off his shoes and bounced on the mattress. The dressing table rattled. The floorboards groaned. The wardrobe door fell halfway open. "Christ, it's like a train's coming through," he said. He cupped his hands and shouted at the ceiling: "The next train to arrive at platform Billy will be the 3:45 for Skeggy. All aboard!" He bounced again. The boards sprang a brad. "Fancy a day out in Skeggy, kiddo?"

"No," I said, as flat as the wall. I was there with Dad, not very long ago. I remember coming home in the pouring rain. And what we found.

And what we didn't.

Graeme laughed and unwrapped a fresh pack of ciggies. He lit up, shook the match and tossed it on the sill. It landed next to the dying cactus. "Want one?"

Course not. Grandad would kill me. "Nana doesn't like people smoking upstairs."

"Then we'll open a window, won't we?" he said. "Either way, the old girl's not gonna know." He leaned forward and gave me his threatening glare. Dark glassy eyes. Short brown lashes. That stripe of bristles he calls a moustache.

"Why did you leave Prestonne School?" I said.

He picked up a paperweight and weighed it in his hand: Uncle Billy's souvenir from White Scar Cavern. "I wanted to better myself," he said, not really saying anything at all. He jiggled the paperweight and lobbed it on the bed. "You're shitting yourself about Prestonne, aren't you?"

Any day now we'd know about the scholarship. Just the thought of it made me sick. "What happened to Frankie? What did they do to him?"

He coughed and swung his feet up onto the bed,

letting his head fall back against the pillow. "Why? You feeling sorry for him now?"

I looked at the floor. I didn't answer that.

He smiled and blew smoke through a parting of his lips. "Forget Lennox. It's all been taken care of."

"What do you mean?"

"He's history. Gone."

"Did he get punished?"

"Oh yeah," Graeme said. "Stripped to the waist. Nine strokes of the lash."

They *hit* him. He was flogged? Like a pirate? No way.

"Roasted him over a spit as well."

They could do that at Prestonne? "You're lying," I said.

"You'll find out when you put on the blazer."

"You don't know, do you?"

"I know plenty," he said.

"So why won't you tell me?"

"Why won't *you* stop being an irritating twat?"

And there it was again. That change of tone. From a taunt to a threat in a single breath. "You can't talk to me like that."

"Oh, gonna run and tell Grandad, are you?"

"I could get you the sack."

"I doubt it," he said. His mouth rolled into a confident sneer. "Since Billy went planting flags on mountains, I'm the old man's favourite twist. I practically run this frigging joint. Your dad's useless – a mess. And you're a liability. Me, the cars and a few wooden boxes are the only things that work round here."

"Get stuffed!"

"Wo!" He spluttered with laughter. "Blimey, I'm almost impressed. The little cavalier's got spunk after all." He picked up one of my football boots and stubbed his fag out between the studs. "I heard Frankie's a good-looking boy."

"So?"

"So maybe you fancy him a bit?"

That was it. I jumped up, planning to run. He caught hold of my arm and hauled me back.

"Get off me!"

"Sit down."

"Get off me, I said!"

We wrestled, but he was always too strong. "Shut up and *sit down*." He threw me backwards onto my bed. "What you need is a sense of humour – or a bloody good clip round the ear. And don't think I wouldn't; it's only your word against mine, after all. Get used to the fact that *I'm* the top monkey around here now. Trust me, you could have worse people sharing this pit. We've probably got more in common than you think." He nodded at one of the boxes he'd brought. "Open that."

No way. I shook my head.

He snorted quietly and dropped to his knees. "How many toys have you got in your cupboard?"

Toys? None. That part of me vanished when my mother walked out.

He tutted and threw back the flaps of the box. "There," he said. "What do you think of them?"

And there was his secret. His passion. His love.

The box was full of soldiers. Model soldiers. Knights of old, in plastic armour.

Put together and painted by him.

FIFTEEN

At home, it was getting to breaking point.

Dad changed his rota so he didn't work Fridays.

And Philip didn't come calling any more.

My mother was like an iceberg, then. Above water, she was visible – present, but cold. Below, we could all feel the currents shifting.

The day before it happened, the day before she went, I heard her in the bedroom, arguing with Dad. It was dusk. I was out in the garden with Bruce, training him over my high jump bar. He cocked his ears at the sound of Mum crying and stared at the room with his tail held stiff.

I shut him in the kitchen and made my way up. On the steps before the landing, I stopped and turned. I peered through the bars of the banister rails.

Their room was open. Poorly lit. Fear, like the sickly

yellow light from the lamps, was draining out, dripping through the fabric of the house. Mum was on the bed with her arms around the girls.

Suddenly a voice said, "Where's the money?" and Dad came storming into view. "Marlene," he said again, "where's the *money*?"

And I couldn't understand this. I just didn't get it. He was standing over Mum with one hand raised and there were banknotes sprouting from his tightly-clenched fist. When he moved them from one hot palm to the other he made them smack with the pressure of his thumb. Like he was being the banker at Monopoly.

But this was not Monopoly.

This was real.

"*Where's the bloody money?*" he screamed.

The power of it flattened me against the wall. I was frightened. I didn't know what to do. I'd never seen rage in my father before. He shook his fist and threw the banknotes down. He clawed at his face as they floated to the floor. The groan of a wounded bear came out of him. His hands spread upwards into his hair. His teeth were so gritted I thought they would crumble. Blue veins pulsed at his straining temples. A teardrop cut across his unshaved cheek. He was changing, going through a kind of transformation. A weredad, howling at an unseen moon. As I stood there shaking I told myself this: any minute now he'll rip off this skin and show me the real Dad underneath.

Any minute now.

Any second.

Now.

"Sixty miserable bloody pounds." There was so much sorrow in his voice. So much. "Where the hell is it? Where's the rest?"

He kicked the dressing table. Kicked it hard. It cracked against the wall. Mum's perfumes toppled. Everything crashed to the pale pink carpet. The scents of her life. Her hair brush. Her earrings. Her dignity. Her marriage. Her future with Dad. Down in the pile with her dressing gown and slippers.

And six crumpled tenners.

And some handwritten letters.

And I still hadn't moved from my place on the stairs. In the kitchen, in the distance, I could hear Bruce barking. 'Eve of Destruction' was playing on the radio. My high jump bar was still on its poles. And I wanted to reach out and step between them. I wanted to give each of them a hand to hold.

But it was my father's hand that rose up first. I saw the clenched fist at the side of his head. I knew the strength in his driver's arms. How many boxes of shoes he could lift. How many bones he could break with a punch.

"Dad!"

My voice was enough to save her. He saw me and staggered out onto the landing. He sank down, gripping the banister rails, pressing his forehead tight against the bars. And all he could say through his tears was this: "I wasn't going to do it. I wasn't going to do it."

Behind him, my mother was reaching out to me. Pleading for something, but I didn't know what.

"What is it?" I shouted. "What do you want?"

Was it me? My love? My father?

Or forgiveness?

SIXTEEN

My grandmother baked me a celebration cake. A Victoria sponge with bright white icing. It still looked wet beneath the kitchen lights, still held the smell of the warmth of the oven. She'd done whorls around the edge to make it look fancy. In the centre, blue and yellow, the badge of Prestonne.

I had to make the first cut, she said.

She wiped the blade of a knife against her apron, turned it round and offered me the handle.

Empty green plates. Paper serviettes. My dad and my grandad waiting for their slice.

I glanced at Graeme, tilting back in his chair. Hands behind his head. Tongue in his cheek. Evening newspaper open on his chest. I knew what he was thinking. His smirk said it all. Weeks ago, Frankie had made the first cut.

I drove the knife into the heart of Prestonne.

"Steady on," said Grandad, jerking back. He flicked a chip of icing off his black silk tie. "You're cutting the bloody thing, not killing it."

"Len, don't swear," my grandmother said. "Are we all for a piece?"

"Aye," said Graeme. He righted his chair and pushed his plate forward. "Who'd have thought we'd have a scholar in the house. You must be proud of the boy, then, Neville?"

"I don't know where he gets it from," said Dad. And the air became still, as if a gong had been struck. All we heard for a moment was the hum of the fridge and Ginger panting at the head of the table.

"What the heck," said Graeme. "He's got your looks. How long before the posh girls want some, eh?"

"That's enough of that," my grandad said. He tapped the table with a jaundiced finger. "I won't have any coarse talk from you. He's at Prestonne to study, not moon over girls."

"There aren't any girls at Prestonne," I said. But no one was taking any notice of me.

"All I meant was, he's at that age," said Graeme, curling the words like smoke around his tongue.

"What age?" I said.

"Never mind," said Nana. "That's enough about girls. Just cut the cake into five neat pieces."

"A pentagram," said Dad.

Graeme gave a quick whistle. "What's this, then, Neville: geometry class?"

Dad turned a penny through his fingers and shrugged. "I had some training as a draughtsman, once."

"Aye, and you gave up too bloody early."

We all looked at Grandad, Ginger included.

"Don't spin that record again," said Dad. His fingers made a spider trap around his nose. He was hurt, I could tell. Stabbed in the heart. You could almost see his past seeping out of the cut.

"You could have had a decent career," said Grandad. "Same with the football, you chucked that away."

"I was injured," said Dad. He showed his palm. "I couldn't play the game on one knee, could I?"

"It wouldn't be your clutch knee, then?" said Graeme.

"You what?" said Dad, as if he might clout him.

"Trials for Derby, Port Vale and Forest," Grandad cracked one knuckle for each. "And you end up carting shoes in a van."

"Len," Nana said.

But the knife was in.

Dad thumped the table. He rose to his feet. His chair legs scraped across the kitchen tiles. "I like driving, all right?" He lost a gob of spit. It pooled on the tablecloth, north of the cake.

"Neville, sit down." Nana pressed his shoulder.

But Dad was strong and stood his ground. He barked at Grandad, "I'll never be bloody well good enough, will I?"

"You had chances is all I'm saying."

"No, that's not half of what you're saying," said Dad. "Let's hear the rest of it. Let's have it all. No wonder she left me. No wonder she walked. The grass was greener. I let my kids down."

"You had chances, that's all I'm saying, Neville."

"I thought I had love!" my dad shouted out. "I thought that was all I needed, Dad!"

And he stormed into the hall. And my hand was on the knife. And my Nana said, "For God's sake, Len. For God's *sake*." She hurried after Dad. Ginger whined and barked. He wagged his tail and gulped at the cake. Grandad sighed and looked at his watch. He went out, fishing for his cigarette case.

"Seventy-two degrees," said Graeme.

"What?" I said. My head was reeling.

"If you cut a circle into five, you ponce, each slice wants to be seventy-two degrees. It's called division. I thought you were brainy?"

"I don't want to be *brainy*." I wanted to be happy. I slapped the knife handle, making it quiver.

Graeme clamped a fist on it, stopping it dead. "Look at me. *Look at me*," he said with a growl. "You need to get your head straight. You need to get a grip. Better ask yourself what you really want to be: a useless, whinging, beat-up toerag or a knight of Grandmother's oval table?" He pulled the knife clear and showed me the blade. Excalibur, bleeding cream and jam.

"You're mental," I said. "I'm going to see Dad."

"I wouldn't," he said, in his pulling strings voice. He ran his tongue along the knife blade, hilt to tip. "Daddy needs to be with his mummy just now. Oops, there's that nasty word again: mummy. The never-to-be-mentioned Miss Scarlet Taboo. Looks like they're all deserting you, kiddo. No mum. No dad. No *chums* from school. Billy No-mates, that's what you are. And the mutt only wants you for a piece of cake."

"No, he doesn't," I said. "Ginger, come."

"Here, dog," said Graeme, clicking his fingers. Ginger was instantly at his knee, magnetised by a piece of icing.

"You're gonna get picked off," Graeme said. "The

weakling, the calf at the edge of the herd. That's what you'll be at Prestonne: a loser, unless you start learning – *real* fast."

"Learn what?" I said. "More boring kings?"

Every night, in our room, he gabbed about history. He would lie on his bed, in his dressing gown and socks, painting his models and quoting dates.

England. The throne. As if it all mattered.

As if I might care.

As if I couldn't sleep.

But that day he said, "No, not kings." He drove the kitchen knife back into the cake, cracking the surface like an Arctic icebreaker. "I'm gonna teach you survival," he said. "Stuff from the great big School of Life. I'm gonna change your way of thinking. I'm gonna turn you into a *man*."

Now he had that look in his eye again. That dark, treacherous, secretive glint. He put a chunk of icing into his mouth, letting it ride on the wave of his tongue. "Lesson one tomorrow. We'll start with Gina."

"Who's Gina?" I said.

His gaze dipped somewhere below my waist. And he took another crumb or two of cake – and smiled.

SEVENTEEN

On the morning after the row about money, I wake to a cold hand clamping my ankle.

Dad raises one finger up to his lips. In a whisper he says, "There's toast on the table. Marmalade, too."

It's our code. Our secret agent's greeting. He means he's going to take me in the van today.

But it's Saturday–?

He raises the finger again. "Agents don't ask questions," he says.

Then he does something he's never done before. He leans over and puts a kiss on my forehead. He smells of the sofa. Night sweats. Bruce. He smells of everything I love about my dad.

He walks his fingers.

I nod. I'll be quiet.

He shows me five.

I'm there in four.

We have marmalade on toast in the moonlit kitchen. Then we're out in the rain with the foxes in the darkness, to the top of the estate where the van is parked.

In the cab, I tell him, "Dad, I'm scared." I wanted to tell him this last night. But we were sent to bed early, malt in our cocoa, something to make us sleep and forget.

"Scared?" he says.

"Why was Mum crying?"

He fires up the van. It takes two tries. It rumbles as if we're a Saturn Five rocket, as if we're going to fly away into space. "Guess where we're going?"

Could it be Saturn? Could it be space? I look at the stars. The pale blue stars. At the hunter, Orion, standing above us. Sometimes, I'd like to be up there with him, sitting at his left foot, shining bright. "Dad—?"

"Okay, I'll give you a clue." He cuts right across me in a weird edgy voice that sounds likes it's coming from a cage within his chest. "Cabbages. Brussels sprouts. Thousands of them."

"Skegness?" I say. And I'm suddenly excited. I start thinking of the seashore, ice creams, slot machines, the crazy golf course where we all played pirates.

Dad smiles. He chews on the side of his thumb. The van bumps a kerb.

And we're on our way.

Skegness, though? It's not on the northern run. I'm not even sure they have shoe shops there. Anyway, it's Saturday. We don't deliver Saturdays.

"Dad—?"

"Let's have a biscuit," he says. He taps a lunch box lying on the seat between us. There's a half pack of ginger creams. Sandwiches. Fruit. A thermos flask and two stout cups. Everything we need for a grand day out. He punches a button on the radio receiver. A gloomy, rather posh voice fills the cab. *Cold and rain, spreading right across the east.* Dad says, "Don't pay attention to that. The sun always shines when we go to Skeg." He winds down his window and checks his mirror. The wipers sweep the rain aside, smearing dirt across my line of vision. We're on Meadowcliffe Road now, passing the house. Dad doesn't seem to care or notice. But I do. I see things he doesn't.

A hard yellow light in my bedroom window.

The tall, soft shadow of my mother by the curtain.

A sparrow alone on the telephone wire.

On the way to Skegness we talk about football. We

laugh, we eat fruit, we play 'Name Ten Things'. Dad tells me about his time in the navy. The duties he carried out on aircraft carriers. He doesn't ask about people at the house any more. And if I talk about Mum, he just changes the subject.

He parks the van on the open seafront. The radio was right and Dad is wrong. The sun isn't shining; the rain hasn't stopped. It's slanting side-saddle on the wind, blurring the view of the town and beach. One gust shudders the skin of the van. Gulls cry murder. The grey sea rolls. Everything smells of layers of salt. The clock tower has its hands at eight. Dad's hands are gripped to his steering wheel. When I ask what he's staring at he just says, "Nothing. Come on, let's chase the tide."

So we struggle down the beach, my father and me, with our heads in our chests and our hands in our pockets, splashing in the runnels that form between the sandbanks. It's cold. The sea is a long way out. Soon I can't feel my ears and nose. My feet are wet, my socks are pulp, my green anorak is soaked in patches. Dad is further ahead than me, in his working overalls and sheepskin coat, striding out to the water's edge. He chases the tide, but it doesn't chase him. It turns and catches him in its sway. Soon, the sea has covered his boots. And he still hasn't stopped. Still he keeps walking. And I know that the water is strong and cold and I'm frightened that the sea will steal him away. So I splash through the tide because I want to save him. I crash into his back and tug at his coat. *Dad? Dad? What are we doing?* And he pulls me round to stand in front of him. He turns me so we're looking at the sea together, clamping me firmly against his body. We're ankle deep and the rain is hitting and my father says, "Look at it. Look out there. This is all there is for you and me now."

And I don't know what he means. And I don't know what we're doing. Skegness was never like this before. There is water all over Dad's shaken face. Pearls on his eyebrows. Drops from his nose. Mist in the curly black locks of his hair. In a mumble he repeats to me, "This is all there is." Then his hands slide up to rest on my shoulders and his thumbs come together at the back of my neck. His fingers glide gently inside my collar. "Why didn't you tell me about Philip?" he says.

And all I can do is cry into the sea.

This is when Mr Gordon appears. He calls out, "Hallo, there? Are you all right?"

I break away from Dad and run towards him. He's

tall, angular, older than Dad. Country hat. Mackintosh. Walking stick. Moustache that looks like a vacuum attachment. He points the stick at a floppy-eared spaniel lolloping through the rolling water.

The dog jumps up and nuzzles my hand.

"Don't let him get you wet," says Mr Gordon. He smiles at his slightly silly joke.

"What's his name?" I ask as I rub my eyes.

"Oliver," he says. "You can run with him on the beach, if you like?"

I'd like to. I'd like to run with his dog. But I'm sad and confused and Mr Gordon can see that. He nods. His glance travels sideways to Dad. "Morning."

Dad doesn't speak or want to look up. He stares at the waves and sways a little.

Mr Gordon drills his stick into the sand. He peers towards the grey horizon for a moment. "These tides – strangely deceptive," he says. "Been caught out by them many a time. But maybe not as badly as you have, eh?"

And even I can tell he's forgiving Dad for whatever he thought he was doing in the water.

Mr Gordon introduces himself. He's a local. Dog-lover. Restaurant owner. He can rustle up the finest lemon sole in town. Maybe we'd like to join him for breakfast? Dry ourselves down? Get warm? Eat?

Dad shakes his head. He wades clear of the sea. "We have to go," he says.

Mr Gordon frowns. "You're soaking, man."

"We have to go," says Dad. "I have to take the boy home to his mother."

"Dad, we only just got here," I say. I kick a ridge of sand, making Oliver bark.

But Mr Gordon seems to be satisfied now. Glancing at the van he says, "Yes. Of course. Drive carefully. Be sure to put something warm around him." He nods at us both and calls Oliver away.

Dad does drive carefully, silently, home. By the time we're there I'm nearly asleep. We park in the same place and walk the estate with a map book keeping the rain off our heads. The garden gate is already off the latch, but Bruce starts barking in time to our steps. Dad turns his key. We go into the house. He shouts, "Marlene?" But there is no response.

"Marlene?"

He throws his voice up the stairs.

"Marlene?"

Her name catches deep in his throat.

"Marlene?"

The house is an empty wrapper.

"Marlene. Marlene."

He sinks to his knees.
But she's gone, taking my sisters with her.
And she hasn't even left the heating on.

EIGHTEEN

Gina was his girlfriend. A dot of a thing. Barely at his shoulder, even standing in her heels. He brought her to the house one Sunday afternoon, made a big fuss of her, called her his 'bird'. We had tea and a plate of biscuits together: me, Graeme, Gina and Nana. Out on the plastic chairs on the lawn.

Gina was polite. Quiet and polite. She sat with her legs crossed, slanted at the ankles. One hand was never far from the hem of her skirt, the other hand played with her small, silver cross. She wasn't pretty, not like Audrey Hepburn. Her eyes were small. Her cheeks were round. She had this habit of tilting her head so her hair curled under her chin on one side and fell away showing her earring on the other. Her skin was pale, like vanilla ice cream. When the sun came out she put on a pair of large dark glasses and undid the buttons on the jacket of her suit. Between the buttons of her blouse I could see a row of lace.

Flowers of lace.

All against her skin.

When asked, she took a walk round the garden with Nana. They talked about the strawberries. The time of year. The aphids. The runner beans. The view of Blackpool Tower. Gina slipped off her grey court shoes and toddled round happily at Nana's pace. Nana seemed to like her.

So did I.

"Go on," said Graeme, "you're allowed to look." He'd been watching me, over the barrel of a fag. I'd been trying not to stare. But he knew that, of course.

He blew a great chisel of smoke into the sky. "Tasty, isn't she?"

I stared at him blankly.

"Christ, you don't know jack shit, do you?"

He put his stockinged feet on the chair beside mine.

"They smell," I said. There were holes in them, too.

"Everything ripens in the summer," he said. He changed his position and dropped them in my lap, wedging one heel between the fat of my thighs. He pushed the hard sole of his foot into my crotch, holding it there till I caught my breath.

From the opposite side of the lawn Nana said, "Is everything all right? What are you pair doing?"

She could see me gripping the arms of the chair.

Gina looked at Graeme, and then at me.

"Bit of rough and tumble, that's all," Graeme shouted.

Nana turned Gina to the sweet pea plants.

Graeme flexed his foot again to get my attention. "Ever been seriously kicked in the nuts?"

Accidentally, once, playing soccer with Stevie. The pain had left me throwing up bile.

He read my face. "Well don't act cocky. All I asked was a civil question. What do you think of Gina, eh?"

I lifted my shoulders and dropped them again. "She's a girl," I said, thinking this was stupid.

"She's a woman," he corrected me. "Check out the rear. You won't see anything cuter round here. Go on. Have a butcher's. Gina won't mind. She's a bit of a nympho. They all are, really."

I looked at her bum. It was smooth and curved. Her zip was slightly undone at the waist.

"Well?" he said.

I made a gesture of annoyance. She had a bum. Two cheeks. Don't we all? So what?

"Jesus." He flicked his fag across the lawn. "What

have you got in those balls, fresh air? Isn't there *anything* about her you like?"

"Why?" I was getting mad with him now.

"I'm curious," he said, almost grinding his teeth. "What about her face?"

She was smiling, gathering her hair behind her ear.

"Do you think she's pretty?"

She was crushing something between her fingers. Lemon balm. Nana's favourite herb. "Yes," I admitted, so I wouldn't upset him. Pretty, yes – but not like Audrey. Gina was sort of…kinder to look at. "I like it when she talks."

"Talks?" He looked surprised. "She's blonde," he said.

"I mean, like, when she does this with her mouth." I showed him the way she pouted her lips, as though she was kissing every word she spoke.

He grunted at that and clicked his tongue. He reached for a tissue wedged under her saucer. On it was the pattern of Gina's mouth. "Ever kissed a girl?"

Nothing that didn't have a hairy lip, no.

"Gina, she tastes like honey," he said. "Try it. On this. Go on, I won't be jealous. Don't worry, the lipstick rubs off easily."

I shook my head and tried to push his foot away.

"I'm gonna call Nana if you don't get off." I could feel his body heat pulsing through the sock.

He let his toes curl again, using them like fingers. "You don't have to be ashamed of *that*," he said.

"Nana," I gasped.

And he kicked me over.

"What's going on there?" Nana called. She was distant, busy with Gina and the flowers.

Graeme said, "Bit of man to man. I won."

"Graeme, don't hurt him," Gina said quietly. There was something unforgiving in her light green eyes.

"Me? Wouldn't hurt a fly," he said. And he took my hand and hauled me to my feet, brushing loose grass off the arms of my jumper. He pulled me into shape and patted my cheek. "Say a word and I'll talk to Mr Gifford," he whispered.

Then he ruffled my hair and walked into the house.

NINETEEN

Dad wanted me to go out into the garden. Practise the high jump. Walk the dog. But I couldn't walk away from him. Not just then. I just stood in the front room doorway and watched.

He opened the sideboard. He opened the drawers. He dragged everything down to the front room floor, spilling what was left of her onto the rug. Aprons. Cutlery. Coasters. Napkins. Knitting patterns. Needles. Boxes of threads. The shillings for the meter. The photo albums. The box of Christmas ornaments (fairy lights, the lot). The spare set of tea towels. The posh set of glasses. Recipes. String. Paper clips. A torch. The trophy she'd won for the Civil Service quiz. Envelopes and paper. The sherry decanter.

Then he spilled the empty sideboard too.

He turned the chairs and the settee over, lowered the

mast of the standard lamp. He swept her record player into the alcove, pushed the television onto its back. Into this debris he cried his tears. Colossal sobs from pumping lungs that brought Mrs Allenby, the neighbour, running. She took a breath that the nicotine hadn't yet claimed, put a hand to my head and pressed me to her shoulder.

"She's gone," said Dad. Over and over.

She's gone. She's gone. She's gone. She's gone.

I could hear Mrs Allenby's heart at work, her rib cage rattling against my ear. "Left in a taxi at two," she said. Her words were harsh. All sympathy buried. She blew smoke down her nose. It settled in my hair. "I'm taking the boy next door for a bit."

"No," I said.

She yanked me away. "Your mother had words. Instructions. Come on."

"I don't care," I said. I lashed out at her. I only wanted to be with my dad.

But Mrs Allenby was having none of that. She clipped my ear and dragged me outside. Right away, I heard the back gate thump.

"Bruce," I called. He made a sound like a gas ring setting alight.

"Bloody monster," Mrs Allenby said. "If that were

on the moors, they'd shoot the bloody thing."

"Bruce!" I called again.

He barked and clawed the panels.

Mrs Allenby pinned my shoulders to the wall. "Listen to me, you silly little sod. You're to phone your mother. I said I'd see to it. You talk to her, then I'm washing my hands. I'm washing my hands of it, do you understand? You're all a bunch of dirty, bed-hopping buggers. This estate'll go up in smoke one day."

And she bundled me into fag ash city. The house of a thousand stubs, Dad called it. But Mrs Allenby was posh by Meadowcliffe standards. She had carpets with underlay, a budgie – and a phone.

"Sick of being a bloody exchange," she said, dialling a number off a slip of paper. "Begged me, she did. For the sake of you: the prodigal bloody whinging son. You tell her to take that animal as well, cos I'm up to here with its barking, all right—? Marlene? Aye, Neville's just back. Yes, with the boy. Yes, he's all right – well, as all right as it's going to get; he's still got arms and legs and a head. Five minutes at most or I send a bill. Here." She thrust the phone in my face. "Talk to her, quick, before your dad comes round. And don't you dare dribble inside the receiver."

"Mum?" I shouted. "Mum, where are you?"

"Be quiet and listen carefully," she said.

"Come home. Dad's chucking things over the floor."

She paused. I heard her breathing in shudders. "I can't come home. What's done is done. I'm leaving your father and I'm going to live with Philip."

"No—"

"Listen. I don't have long. Mrs Allenby has some money for a taxi. She's going to call one to the house, to take you away."

"I don't want to go away!"

"Mrs Allenby knows what to do," she said. "Leave everything behind and get into the cab."

I shook my head. "What about Dad?"

Again, she paused. She could have been crying. "Remember in the kitchen when I asked who you'd go with if we ever split up – and you said you'd come with me? That's all I'm asking: come with me."

"No," I said.

Her voice went faint. "Don't be silly, now. You've got to come with me."

I dragged the phone down to the level of my neck.

"Are you there? Can you hear me?"

Mrs Allenby frowned.

I thought about my father, slumped to his knees. I thought about Philip, crushing my hand. I thought about the empty bonbon bags. Then I lifted the phone again and told my mother straight: "I want to stay with my dad."

And I gave the phone back to Mrs Allenby.

She listened to the cries coming out of it a second, then laid it shakily back onto its rest.

"God help you," she whispered, and fished in her purse. She put a pound note in my hand and closed it. "God help you," she said again, and showed me to the door.

TWENTY

One dinnertime, as the summer went on, Graeme made a surprise announcement. "I think I might have to move out." He jabbed his fork at a cluster of chips, using them to mop up the sauce on his plate.

"Oh?" said Nana, pouring tea. She wiped the cracked spout with the end of a cloth.

"Gina's got her eye on a property," he said. "Small terrace, up in Wendlemoor."

Nana put the teapot down on the coaster. "Can you afford it? Houses up there...?"

"Gina's done the necessary sums," said Graeme. "Told me what I'll owe. Where it'll hurt. That's what comes of courting a bird who's climbing the rungs of the estate agent's ladder. She's got inside knowledge. First pick of the crop. Wants to make an honest man of me, I reckon."

Silently, I bit off the end of a chip.

"Will you marry her?" said Nana. "She's a lovely girl."

"Sugar," said Graeme, pointing at the bowl.

I pushed it towards him.

He lumped four spoonfuls into his mug. "Marry her? Crikey. There's a proposition. She can turn a man's head, it's true, can Gina. But I don't think I'm ready to tie the knot yet. I'd rather live in sin for a bit."

"Hey, not in front of him," said Nana.

Graeme sat back and crossed himself.

"And don't take the church in vain," she said.

Not that he'd take any notice of that.

"When are you going?" I said.

He gave a quick snort. "Not soon enough, by the sound of it. You'll be in that bed before the sheets are cold, you will."

"It's Uncle Billy's bed," I reminded him sharply.

He sat forward again and stirred his tea. "Not while there's a knight of King John on the pillow." We hovered together, over the table, my eyes in his, his eyes in mine, like we were readying to go to war.

"Biscuit?" said Nana, opening the tin.

"No, ta," said Graeme. "Watching the figure." He patted his stomach. It was as flat as a board. "Do you want to come and see it?" he said to me suddenly.

"The knight?" I said.

"The house, you berk. Gina's got full permission to view. We're going up there when I've finished my tea. Nice patch of wasteland out to the rear. We could take the dodgy football and the wheezy dog. Let him run off some of that fat."

"He's not fat," said Nana.

"He's a wobbler," said Graeme, bloating his cheeks. To my shame, I almost laughed at that. "What do you reckon, eh? Fancy a ride?"

"Go on," said Nana. "It'll do you good. Better than moping about round here."

"Like you have done all bloody summer," Graeme added.

Billy No-mates. He was right about that.

He thrust his arm forward and checked his watch. "Meet me on the forecourt in twenty minutes. Doesn't do to keep a girl waiting."

"Not if she can do it to you," said Nana.

Graeme laughed and toasted her with his mug. "Nice cuppa is that."

He took a noisy slurp – then left it on the table, unfinished.

TWENTY-ONE

So this is how it is. The way the story goes. I'm riding in the Zephyr with Graeme and his girl. I'm on the back seat with the two of them in front. We don't have the football or the wheezy dog. The radio is on. The windows are down. The sky is huge and silver-blue. I'm wearing my Man United football jersey. Graeme is in his gold-rimmed shades. Gina's in a pair of blue denim shorts and a white crop top and sandals with tan straps that cross around her ankles. She's sitting with her feet on Alice's dash, studying a local A to Z.

Graeme looks across at her. "We don't need that."

She steers the book around like it's her who's got the wheel. "You drive a hearse, not a taxi. You'll get us all lost. Go right at these lights."

He grins and passes her a long limp fag. A *here's one I rolled a little earlier* brand. "I know Wendlemoor.

Mate of mine lives there."

Gina takes a drag and gives the fag back.

"Hey, Boy Wonder, fancy a blow?" Graeme's eyes flick upwards, into the mirror. He shows me the fag. It's almost through. The scent is pressing on my chest so much that it feels like someone's ironing my lungs.

"Graeme?" Gina throws him a questioning look.

"Since when did you grow wings?" he says. "'S'all right. We've got an understanding, me and him. I'm teaching him stuff. I'm grooming him in the ways of the world."

She rolls her head and looks over her shoulder. Her eyes are red. She doesn't look pretty. "You smoke?" she says.

I don't know what to say. She takes this as an admission of guilt.

"You bad bugger," she says with a silly little giggle. She takes the fag again. "None of this, all right?"

"Let him try it," says Graeme. He scratches his wrist. He has red patches, eczema, on his fair-haired arms.

"He's a kid," says Gina. She sounds disapproving.

Graeme's black shades fill the width of the mirror. "Kids grow up pretty fast these days."

"I'm not surprised, sharing a room with you." She puts a hand across her breast and coughs like a duck.

It's easy to tell that she doesn't smoke much. "So what have you been telling him, then?" she asks.

"The stuff all lads want to know," says Graeme. His hand reaches over and strokes her thigh. "Though some things are better from the mouth of a woman."

For some reason, he puts his tongue in his cheek.

"Graeme, he's just a frigging kid," she says.

And I'm shocked, not because I've heard her swear. It's the fear in her voice that's turned me cold. Like she's suddenly worked out why I'm coming for the ride. Like she knows the kind of hold that Graeme has on me.

Mr Gifford doesn't like namby-pambies.

Mr Gifford likes fine young men in his care.

Mr Gifford likes boys who look up to him, says Graeme.

One word to Mr Gifford and my life at Prestonne Grammar will be hell.

Gina moves his hand back onto the wheel, telling him to keep his thoughts on the road. As it happens, we're almost at our journey's end. Graeme swings Alice into Upper Meade Road, bumping off the kerb by a row of terraced houses. It's a decent neighbourhood. A sleepy cat street. Trees pitching shadows. Large bay windows. Just like the road that Philip used to live on.

"Hey, kid, why don't you take a walk?" says Gina.

The idea isn't appealing. I'm not sure my feet would

know what to do. I feel light-headed. Wuzzy. Strange. Like a blurry television that needs a good thump. Gina's face seems suddenly softer to look at. Her eyes are like melted mint ice cream. While I'm thinking what to say to her Graeme leans sideways, reaching into Alice's glove compartment. He pulls out a model of a knight on horseback. "I brought the kid here so he could see the house."

"And why've you brought *that*?" Gina says, looking dazed.

"For the vibe," he says. He sounds a little drunk.

Gina shakes her head and fiddles in her bag. She separates one of two keys from a ring. "There's a park up there on the left," she says. "Give us half an hour. Number 9, okay?"

She dangles the key. Graeme snatches it up. He's dangerous now, like a mazy wasp. "I said, he's coming into the house."

"No," she says, bleary but capable. "Not until *we've* had a look round first." Calmly, she hands me the other key.

An ice cream van goes trundling past. I figure it's a good enough excuse to leave. So I fall out and follow its jangling song. For minutes that seem to pass more like hours I'm chasing it round the curving road. And all the while I'm trembling lightly, like I've stepped from the bath on a winter's day. My hairs are raised but I don't know why. I feel guilty, even though I've done nothing wrong. I've barely spoken since we left Nana's house. A fact not lost on the ice cream man. He has to ask me twice, "What kind of cornet?"

He's Mario. He has a Manchester accent. Scar on his lip. I show him my money.

He scrapes it into his black leather pouch, tells me straight I won't get a flake.

As it happens, I don't get the ice cream either. While his back is turned and he's digging in the tub, I see two figures nearing the van. They're both in brown shades, T-shirts, shorts.

One has a wave of bright blond hair.

I'm halfway down the road before Mario calls. I can't hear any other voice but his, but I know what Frankie will be saying to him. 'So what? Leave it. I'll take that.'

Near to Alice, I think about trying her doors. I hover. Panic. Change my mind twice. I'm pretty sure Frankie didn't see me run, but if he comes here, he'll have me like a fly in a bottle. I need a castle. A hideaway. Four strong walls. Something solid that he can't blow down.

So I use the key to number 9, Upper Meade.

The house smells lonely. Bare grey boards. Sunlight is a ghost that doesn't walk here. But in the shuddering dust there is always sound. I hear footsteps. Graeme's. At the top of the stairs. He's stripped to the waist and there's something in his hand. It looks like the knight from the glove compartment.

"You're early. Brought me a ninety-nine?"

A joke, but I still sense menace in his voice. In the background I think I hear Gina sobbing. "Frankie's outside. What's the matter with Gina?"

He comes down the stairs, barefoot, like a monk. "Frankie?" His gaze rolls into the distance. "Oh, yeah. The lion in Daniel's den." And I don't understand this, but Graeme clearly does. He laughs as if gas has been pumped through his lungs. Then his gaze swings back to his hands and he says, "Look at it. Look at this. Look what she did."

He must mean the knight. The lance is in half. One of the horse's legs is snapped.

"1264," he mutters blankly.

A history lesson? With Frankie on the prowl? Again I ask, "What's the matter with Gina?" She's definitely crying. It's scaring me now.

The stairs creak as he drops down another two steps,

caressing the horse's armoured mane. "Simon de Montfort. Earl of Leicester. Took the throne from Henry III. First full battle fought with lances." He looks at me as if this ought to make sense. "She broke my favourite model," he says.

And he hurls it down the hall where it strikes the front door. Simon de Montfort loses his head. But Graeme isn't done with the Earl of Leicester yet. "*She broke my favourite model!*" he screams. He runs down the hall in pursuit of it now. Then he pulls the door open as far as it will go, trapping the model against the skirting, crushing it to pieces with repeated blows.

And now I don't know what's scaring me the most: the open door, the maniac by it, or the gentle sobs I can hear upstairs.

It's there that I run. Upstairs. To Gina.

She's lying on a bed. A single bed. An iron frame. A mattress. Nothing more. Her knees are drawn up, tight under her chin, her pale face covered by a tangle of arms. Her skin is on fire, her shoulder looks bruised. The chain of her silver cross is spilling from her fist. When she hears my voice she extends a hand. "Hold me," she says. "Hold me. Please." She hauls me close. Desperately close. Close enough to let me feel the warmth draining out of her. Close enough to smell her mussed-up hair. But it's only when she turns and her breasts fall forward that I wake up and realise what I'm doing.

I'm hugging a girl for the very first time.

Graeme's girl, Gina.

And she's absolutely naked.

TWENTY-TWO

He was the sort of dad who drew circles of chalk beneath the kitchen window. Targets. For the practising of football skills. Half an hour after school. Extra sessions at the weekend. *Blatt*, against the wall. Trap the rebound. *Blatt!*

Balance. That was the trick, he'd say. Knee over the ball. Shoulder down. Steady. Side foot for accuracy. Instep for power. Hit those circles. Place that shot. Not to worry if the neighbours moaned or the dog began to bark or the rain came down. A professional had to put that out of his head.

And when it became too easy, too sweet, when the arc of the foot was in the comfort zone and moss was growing on the undisturbed chalk, he would rub them out at night and redraw them smaller. Move them around. Make me work.

One day, I would play for the City, he said.

One fine blue day.

For the City.

One day.

He's still on his knees when I run back in from Mrs Allenby's house. Hands on his midriff, pressed in tight. There's so much stuff scattered over the floor that I wonder how the walls and cupboards could have held it. "Dad?" I stumble on a cuddly toy. Charmaine's rabbit. It spills me closer. I have to push a chair aside to get to him still. "Dad?" I lay my hand on his arm. The hand that's still clutching the pound note in it.

The crackle of money makes him turn. "Where'd you get this?"

I tell him straight. Everything that happened at Mrs Allenby's house. Mum's plans to send me away in a cab.

"Taxi? Where to?"

I tell him I don't know.

But he knows that a pound won't get me far.

He rises up like the sea god, Neptune, old photographs draining from the well of his hands. The echo of the deep must be loud in his ears because he doesn't respond to my voice for a second. Then he turns his head and stares at the clock, one of the few things not on the floor. "Go and put a lead on Bruce," he says.

Minutes later, we're both in the van again. Bruce is sitting on the seat between us. This time we head for the city, not the sea. Past the football ground, away from the shops. Along streets too narrow, corners too tight. We roll into a quiet, sloping road where the houses all have large bay windows. Trees catch their branches on the mirrors of the van. The engine shudders to a grateful stop.

"Where are we?" I ask.

Dad looks across the road. He's staring at a house – just a clone of the rest, except for the ivy growing round the door. "Stay in the van, whatever happens."

He slams his fist down hard on the horn, holding it there till passers-by turn. Till Bruce begins to bark. Till curtains twitch.

In the house across the road, a face looks out of the upstairs window.

Philip.

Dad immediately opens his door, throwing it wide against the gravity of the camber. "Bruce, come," he says. The dog can't wait. His tail disappears and the cab door slams.

From the window, Philip is signalling to me. He can't tell, because of the shadow of the trees, if Dad is coming to his door or not.

So I nod, because I want him to know. But I don't know why I want him to know. He looks anxious, sickly. He slicks his hair. He just has time to loosen his tie before he hears Dad hammering hell on his door.

"Open up!" Dad's voice echoes way up the road. He hammers again, then leans back and kicks. The door shudders, but it holds. Dad kicks and kicks. "Open up, you coward! I want my girls!" He looks around the garden and snatches up a pot. No, I'm thinking. But Dad doesn't stop. He plunges the pot through the glass of the door, then fumbles inside and lifts the latch. Now I can see a struggle of sorts. Dad half in, half out of the house. Bruce edging backwards, barking like a demon.

This is the moment I exit the van. To help or to rescue? I'm not really sure. As I run across the road I see Dad and Philip locked in a tussle at the front of the hall. Philip's a tall man, taller than Dad, but he doesn't have a navy man's grit in his gut. Dad punches him, low down, hard in the ribs. Philip buckles, looking hurt. He slumps against the wall. He slides away, clutching at a telephone table. One more glancing blow to the head and he's laid out, groaning, glasses skewed.

Bruce, by now, is at Dad's side, wanting to take some of Philip back home. Dad grabs him before he can make the first bite. He holds him, slavering, by his collar. "Where are they?" he says. "Where are my girls?"

Philip shakes his head. There's blood on his lip. No air in his lungs. No fight in his heart.

"Marlene, bring them down!" Dad shouts. He lets Bruce forward another half inch.

"Not here," says Philip, flinching away.

"Liar," says Dad, and he lets Bruce go.

Suddenly, down the hall, a voice cries, "Daddy!"

"Charmaine?" gasps Dad.

But it's not Charmaine. It's another girl, young, about Charmaine's age.

"Kelly, run," says Philip.

Her screams fill the hall.

And even Dad can recognise the danger now. "Bruce, down!" he yells. The dog has changed direction, readying to strike. Dad vaults over Philip and yanks Bruce back.

Kelly is clinging to the newel post. She's a pretty little girl with flowers on her dress and tears on her face and a broken daddy on the floor of their hall.

She could almost be a parallel image of me.

"Get out," says Philip, struggling to sit. "Get out of my house and leave us alone. Marlene's gone to her mother's, in Sale. I was only supposed to take the boy to her. Get out. Now. Or I'm calling the police."

Dad shakes his head in confusion and defeat. And we both know this is where our old life stops. Right here, in the hallway of Philip's house. The world resets. A new journey begins. Me, my dad and a hungry Alsatian, riding the straight grey motorway north. To a badly-sprung bed in a creaking house. To pocket money, washing down funeral cars. To an alien tongue and an unknown school. To gravel in my palm.

To Frankie Lennox.

PART TWO

at Prestonne

ONE

Day one. Prestonne. The chapel bell is tolling, calling home its pupils, new and old. As we walk up the drive towards the gateway arch, bustling along with a crowd of other boys, I think I might throw up against a stone pillar. Dad's motored on a stride before he knows I've pulled up. It's a teacher, not him, who spots me first.

"Are you all right there, boy?"

He's tall, sharp-eyed, with a drooping moustache. I wouldn't want to take any sweets from him, no matter how respectable he thinks he looks in his striped suit buttoned once at the waist. Near the neck of his tie is a Prestonne pin.

"He's my son," says Dad, coming back into play. "First day nerves. He's new to the school." His hand falls heavily on my shoulder, setting off a low-lying rumble in my guts.

The teacher looks down at me, keeping his distance. He has a kind, but impatient, authority about him, as if he's refereeing a rugby match. He'll be calling for a stretcher if I don't straighten up. "New arrivals should report to the master in reception."

"I take it I should show him this?" asks Dad. He brandishes my letter of acceptance to the school. My passport into Frankie's burrow. My eye checks out the balcony of the quad, wondering if he's up there, watching, waiting.

"Ah, now that's a little different," says the teacher. He checks the letter quickly and steps aside, scanning the herd with resourceful purpose. "He'll need to go to Mr Perry, the lower school head. He'd better have an escort…Thorpe!" His shout makes a fearful dent in the hum. Out of the crowd comes a fresh-faced kid, looking like he just can't wait to serve. He's got a screwed-on smile and Tintin hair: a black quiff shaped like a roll of butter.

"Sir?"

I stare at Thorpe. He grins at me. I've never seen a boy so neatly dressed. The knot of his tie is pebble-smooth and not a millimetre loose in the wings of his collar. There's an iron-sharp crease in his charcoal trousers, teardrop loops in the laces of his shoes. The pockets of his blazer are completely flat, like all he keeps about him is a sheet of paper and the aptitude to multiply a row of fractions. He's Prestonne, pure to the recommended Y-fronts. If he ever needed work, Grandad would employ him to usher the grieving. Me, I'm the kid from the chorus line of *Oliver*: my shirt is stitched, my shoes have holes, and there are folds and sags in the seat of my pants. I'm walking into school in my Uncle Billy's cast-offs. What I wouldn't give to have him here beside me, or for an ounce of his courage right now.

"Hello," says Thorpe.

We shake hands, like we're going to toss a coin for ends. He's posh with an accent so far south that he's surely been dumped here by an alien craft. I like him, though. It's difficult not to.

"Take him to Mr Perry's room," says the teacher as though he's condemned me to eternal detention. I didn't think my pants were as bad as all that.

"Sir," says Thorpe, with military correctness. He pauses and looks at Dad.

This is Dad's moment. His chance to come good. To send me off with words of paternal inspiration. But Dad is away with the fairies again. All summer he's been at the bottom of the garden. And he might as well be sleeping in a plant pot now. He seems mystified and slightly overwhelmed by the splendour. School was never like this for him. He thinks about a handshake, the manly thing to do, but bites the quick of his thumb instead. "Enjoy yourself," he manages to say at last. "Get yourself into the football team."

"Oh good, you play soccer. What position?" asks Thorpe. He's as cheery as a blob of jam in sago.

"Thorpe, get along, boy," the teacher says.

Thorpe clicks his heels and draws me away. We drop into the current of a blue and yellow tide. It sucks us through the gateway, into the quad. Now we're trapped on all sides by baked, red walls. Castellations. Ivy. History in the mortar. The small leaded windows of Old Prestonne School begin to pick me out like a compound eye. In a moment of panic I look back for Dad. He's faded to a head and a distant hand. My heart beats a complex rhythm in my chest.

Some partings you know will always be for ever.

"What's your name?" asks Thorpe.

I can't say right away. His school badge is so shiny it's turning the morning sun into my eyes. I'm also trying to work out why no one is walking on the neatly-mown grass. In the body of the quad lies a lawn half the size of a football pitch, but we're squirting round the edge like bubbles in a pipe.

I tell him my name.

He repeats it to himself. "Good. All the chaps use surnames here."

It would be Lennox, then. Lennox. Not Francis or Frank. I remember it, spluttered out to Uncle Billy. Frankie Lennox. Upper fifth. Blond-haired 'chap' with a dimple in his chin. Silent predator.

Somewhere.

Waiting.

Thorpe drags me onto a cloistered walkway, then through a modern door into the school. Everything smells of polish and wood. And old light fittings. And the leaves of books. The dark brown floorboards throb with an air of discipline and pride. You can see it in the silverware glinting in the cabinets, hear it rushing through the worm-riddled beams. Prestonne. Prestonne. Ra, ra, ra.

Everything about this school is 'ra'.

"Here," says Thorpe. He gives a brisk knock on a half-opened door.

"Come," says a voice.

In a room made small by its overcrowded bookshelves, two teachers are discussing what looks like a timetable. The older one, wispy-haired, in spectacles and gown, glances sideways towards the door. "Yes, what is it?" He flips a sheet of paper over a clipboard, flips it back and hands it to his colleague.

Thorpe explains his errand.

I hand in the letter.

Mr Perry trims me with one stern glance. "Oh yes, that's right, the scholarship boy. Joining us in second year. Most unusual."

"He plays soccer," says Thorpe, as if football is the key to the mysteries of the universe.

"I dare say he does," Mr Perry mutters back.

The second teacher raises a cheerful smile. "If he's good, we'll want to claim him for Latimer." He's shorter than the other man, but quite athletic-looking, what Mum used to call a 'clothes hanger type': stiff arms, round-shouldered, not much neck. A jacket that's a size too small for his chest. Same story with his fingernails and hands. The nails are clipped so deep into the skin that his finger ends look like thermometer bulbs. His hair is steel wool, tight and black. I'm suspecting you wouldn't want to mess with him much, but there's a kindness in his eyes I feel I can trust. So I dare to ask, "What's Latimer – sir?"

"Our house," says Thorpe, jumping in bravely.

"Tudor, Windsor, Stuart and Latimer. We're green, and the best – except at soccer. What position were you again?"

Centre forward. Goalie. Anywhere you like. "Wing half," I tell him. Tribute to Dad. It's what he would have been at Derby County.

"Excellent." The younger teacher squeezes my shoulder. I'm expecting that my collar bone will crush to splinters, but his fingers are almost tender on my muscles. "We could do with shoring up the midfield somewhat. Mr Perry, by virtue of the ancient law of possession – by that, I mean we saw him first, didn't we, Thorpe? – I claim this boy for the Grand House of Latimer."

"Yes, why not," Mr Perry says tiredly. Ten minutes into term and he looks like he'd rather be back in his coffin. He summons up the energy to speak to me again. "Welcome to Prestonne. We don't demand much, just hard work and honesty. This is an academic institution of the highest standard and the best reputation, which we expect our pupils to uphold both inside and outside these walls. We do not tolerate bad behaviour, foul language or poor manners. You will always refer to the masters as 'sir' and treat your fellow students with friendship and respect. You are here to engage in the noble art of learning. Through learning comes achievement. Through achievement comes pride.

"I will leave you in the capable hands of Mr Thorpe. He will show you the ropes and introduce you to your form. If you have any queries or difficulties you may address them to me. Now, morning assembly is almost upon us. Is there anything, briefly, you wish to ask?"

Just one thing, strangely. "Sir, why do you use the name Latimer when it's not a royal house?"

"Good Lord. Well spotted," the other teacher says. There's a twinkle in his eye when he looks at me now. I'm not sure, but it doesn't seem entirely academic. "Where did that spring from? Are you keen on history?"

Mr Perry prompts me with a hopeful eyebrow.

"Yes," I say, trying not to disappoint, even though it's a partial lie. Six weeks in Graeme's company has taught me this much: how to view the world through a cynical eye and how to assess the past in one line: "History is the stuff of murder and betrayal."

"A fair summing up," Mr Perry agrees, parking his thumbs in the slip of his gown.

His colleague, however, seems lost for words, as if he can't believe what his ears just heard. Or maybe they can. For it seems to me he knows this phrase very well. Maybe, he's even spoken it himself.

It's Thorpe who makes the bad penny drop into place. "I love history," he says, with a glow in his cheeks, "and Mr Gifford is the best master going. He runs the lower school soccer team as well."

Suddenly, the floor seems to melt beneath me. This is *Mr Gifford*? Graeme's friend?

He, like me, seems equally thrown. He leans sideways and squints at my letter of acceptance. He can read my name, put a place to my address. The undertaker's boy, on the road towards Chevington. Now I'm beginning to make sense to him.

And suddenly, somehow, he looks unnerved. But he jiggles his tie and says to Thorpe, "Thank you for that vote of confidence, Thorpe. If I ever need a reference I'll know where to come." He lets his gaze rest steadily on me. "To answer your question, Latimer was a sixteenth century martyr, burned at the stake for his religious beliefs. We take his name as our fourth house because the founder of the school, Elijah Prestonne, can trace his ancestry back to the man who allegedly set the torch."

"Gruesome, eh?" Thorpe says, grinning.

This has Mr Perry wincing in despair.

"Sorry, sir," says Thorpe, remembering his place.

Mr Gifford taps the clipboard against his chin. "If you're interested," he says in an even tone, "I run a discussion group after school on a Thursday, where we chat freely about any topic from history. If the content of our curriculum doesn't satisfy your youthful lust for murder, I'd be happy to see you there. It's open to everyone throughout the school. Have a think about it once you've settled in."

On the close of his sentence a fresh bell tolls.

"That's the last call for assembly," says Thorpe.

"Yes, it is," Mr Perry says gratefully. "I'm delighted that six weeks of empty-headed play has not dulled you to the rigours of school routine. Escort your new friend to the Great Hall, please. And see to it he's allocated a locker and a peg."

"Yes, sir," says Thorpe and turns us, quick march, into the corridor.

Straight away we're in the buzz of a crowd of kids, gathering up the pollen of a first day of term. Thorpe is babbling all the way, school protocols and stuff, more football chat. But I'm too dazed to take it in. I'm confused about what I've just seen. Mr Gifford is nothing like the man I imagined. This is the teacher who disciplined Frankie, the friend who drinks at the

Cotton Arms with Graeme, the man who was supposed to make hell of my life if I spoke out of turn about Graeme to Nana.

This is the man who knows about the knife.

"Thorpe, what's Mr Gifford like?"

"Brilliant," he says, as we press towards a group of kids rummaging in lockers.

"Do you go to his group?"

He shakes his head. "Thursday's my French night. *Je m'appelle Adrian*, by the way. It's mostly those from the upper forms, I think."

Like Frankie? How clever is Frankie, I wonder? "If you were sent to him for punishment, would he be strict?"

"All the masters are strict," he says, "but Mr Gifford is definitely the fairest. Everyone calls him 'the lamb' – though not to his face, of course."

He's about to say more when we're stopped in our tracks by a voice along the corridor barking, "Order!" The noise level instantly drops to a murmur, just like someone's turned down the telly.

"That's Jeffers," Thorpe whispers, looking tense. "He's a prefect. They can be worse than the masters. He gave me a shameful mark last term for having dirt in my hair after playing soccer. Always be polite and do what he says. Best to avoid him like the bubonic."

But the boy in front of us hasn't read the script. As he bangs his locker shut it springs back open, attached only by the lower hinge. The upper hinge *chings* as it hits the floor. The damage caused is not intentional, the lockers are wooden and older than Nana, but I can sense by the general intake of breath that there's going to be trouble: Jeffers has seen it.

"Reynolds," he barks. He comes striding down the corridor, face just hidden by the flapping door.

"It just happened, Jeffers," Reynolds says, panicked.

"Defacing school property on the first day of term. That's pathetic, you despicable whelk."

"I'll fix it," says Reynolds, gathering up the hinge. And he shuts the door again, just to prove it will stay.

And that's when I see him, and he sees me. Jeffers: the boy on the road with Frankie.

The one who dropped his fag when I threw my punch.

TWO

For once, I can't wait for Graeme to get in. He swans into the bedroom, late afternoon, pulling off his tie like an outlaw who's just escaped the hangman's noose. "I'm shagged," he says and flops onto his bed. He reaches for a fag from a shirt pocket limp with broken stitching. "Bloke we barbecued this afternoon must have been all of twenty stone. Still got the dent in my collar bone to prove it. Where's my frigging lighter? You got my lighter?" He swings himself upright, fumbling around on the chest of drawers. I wait until he's found a spare lighter in his rammel. Without a thin spout of tobacco in his mouth he can't and won't talk any kind of sense. He drops back, sucking hard on the weed.

"Frankie's mate is a prefect," I tell him.

"Who?"

"Frankie's *mate*. His name is Jeffers."

Graeme sighs and clicks his tongue. He fans a set of smoke rings towards the ceiling. This is how we talk sometimes, in smoke.

He doesn't ask, but I tell him – about my first day. Thorpe. Dad leaving. Latimer House. The quad. The grass thou shalt not walk on, *ra*. The slightly unusual meet with Mr Gifford. The terrifying power of Roland Jeffers.

"Roland?" Graeme laughs at that.

"What do you think I should do?" I ask.

He eases off his shoes, in no rush to answer, wiggles his toe through a hole in his socks. He brings the toe closer, picking at the nail, digging out a curving scoop of dirt. "Keep your nose clean. Stay out of his way."

"He's a *prefect*. He'll find some way to get me."

"So?" Graeme says, like he really couldn't care. "Pulling the wings off flies like you is all just part of the game at Prestonne. What about Lennox? He a prefect too?"

I look away, gripping fistfuls of mattress. "I don't know. I didn't see him." Not even a glimpse. And I could hardly ask Thorpe. "Why did you lie to me about Mr Gifford?"

He looks baffled. "What're you talking about now?"

"I met him. He was kind to me. He knew who I was."

"Oh, aye, he knows who you are," Graeme says, funnelling lines of smoke through his nose.

"Why do people call him 'the lamb'?" It was only after school, on the short walk home, that I remembered I'd forgotten to ask Thorpe about this.

"*Mairrrr*," says Graeme, doing a passable impression of a sheep.

He thinks this is funny. One bleat maybe is.

Mairrrr! Mairrrr!

Now, as usual, he's taking the piss. I'm about to stand up when he finally answers. "His name's Lawrence."

Lawrence? My face turns blank.

"After the TV puppet, thickhead."

Oh, yeah. 'Larry the Lamb'.

"Puppet," Graeme says again, chewing on a smile.

So now I know where the nickname comes from, but I still don't know how Mr Gifford earned it.

Graeme, though, is tired of this now. He crimps his cigarette and leaves it in a saucer with half a dozen more. He swings himself upright, off the bed. "Going for a bath. Seeing Gina tonight."

Gina. It makes me sick to think of them together. Why does she stick with a man like Graeme after the way he treated her? She still turns up at Nana's now and then, as if nothing ever happened at Wendlemoor. But she doesn't talk to me. Not anymore. I'm lucky if she throws a smile my way.

"Going dancing," Graeme says, doing a one-handed jive. "She likes a bit of twist – and shout – does Gina." He chuckles crudely and hitches up his balls, then strips off his shirt and admires his string-vested figure in the mirror. "Give you threepence if you come in and scrub my back."

"Sod off."

I see his reflection smile. He throws his bath towel over his shoulder. Then his shadow falls across me and he lifts my chin. "Don't get cocky," he says very quietly, slapping the hollow drum of my cheek. "You might have grown up a bit over the summer but you're still nothing more than an unflushed turd. Nowt's what it seems at Prestonne. Nowt." Then he backs off, jiving, down the landing, whistling loudly all the way.

THREE

The first casualty of Mum walking out was Bruce.

"The dog's got to go," my grandfather said.

We had driven for hours in the niggling rain, tied Bruce to a drainpipe by the chapel of rest, left him beating his tail in a puddle. And all Grandad can say is: the dog has got to go.

In the kitchen, Dad tried to plead his case. "He'll be all right, Dad. He's a good dog. Trained. He'll earn his ticket guarding the business. Ginger will get used to him. We all will, right?"

"He'll eat poor Ginger alive," said Nana. She ruffled the fur on the spaniel's neck. He turned his matted ears to the window.

"Hark at it," said Grandad, gaunt and stern. "Howling like a bloody wolf, it is."

"He's confused," said Dad.

"Aye, and so are you. We're not a hotel, Neville. Or a bloody kennels. If you're going to live here, you have to fit in. Sacrifices have to be made." He tapped the word 'have' into the kitchen table.

"Grandad, please don't send Bruce away."

But he kept his sagging face primed on Dad, his gaze as straight as the stripes on his waistcoat.

"It's only temporary," said Dad. He bit the side of his thumb. "Anyway, we'll all be back home soon."

Grandad, tight-lipped, took a sharp breath.

My grandmother turned away from the sink. She saw the sadness welling in my eyes and said, "We can't keep Bruce, love. Two dogs. It's too much."

"What about the army?" another voice said. Uncle Billy was sitting on the back doorstep, chipping dried mud off his walking boots. "The dog's young. They might take him. Or the police?"

Glances were swapped. Thoughts exchanged. "Whatever's done, do it quickly," Nana said. She put her hand on the back of my head and pressed me against her flour-stained pinafore.

"All right, I'll look into it tomorrow," Dad sighed.

"No!" I cried.

"That's enough," said Grandad.

I looked at Dad, at the helplessness swimming in

his watery brown eyes.

"Bloody harlot. This is all her fault," said Nana.

And that was the marker. That was the seal. From then on, my mother got the blame for everything.

Next morning, I woke on the spare bed in Uncle Billy's room. The springs were wrecked. My back was hurting. It was like I'd been sleeping in a fruit bowl, a dish. The barking and the howling had stopped outside. Dad and Uncle Billy – and Bruce – had gone. Grandad was doing his accounts in his office. Nana let me have the run of the house.

But I didn't run. Or walk. Or sleep. I lay on the sofa, curled up in silence. Ginger, on the hearth rug, panted and watched. At lunchtime, Nana made a bowl of soup. She stood like a warder while I spooned it down. She ripped hunks of bread from the centre of a loaf. The only words she said were, 'eat' and 'slowly'. When I was done she took the dish away and let me sink into the sofa again. Ginger laid down and went to sleep.

In the mid-afternoon, my father came in.

"Wake up," he said. He rattled my shoulder.

I opened one eye and closed it again. I didn't want to see him. He didn't have my dog. Ginger, my new best friend, sat up.

"I found a good home for Bruce," Dad said. He was still behind the sofa, looking down. There was something in his hands. A box, like a jigsaw.

I turned away, screwing my face into a cushion.

"He's going to be a police dog, catching crooks."

Ginger panted and wagged his tail.

"The police," Dad said again. "I thought you'd be proud."

In the budgie cage, Willoughby spilled some seed.

"Sit up," Dad said, losing his patience. "I want you to stop this. Do as you're told." He shook me again. His touch was light. He wasn't used to this. Bringing up the kids. That was the job of his absent wife.

I swung upright, a stiff-jointed dummy, a doll. I stared at the ash in the fireplace grate. Ginger came up and nuzzled my hand.

Dad put the box on the sofa beside me. A model kit. A Messerschmitt 110. A German plane for a German Shepherd. One corner of the lid was badly crumpled. Yellowed sticky tape was holding it together. He'd ripped off the price tag, leaving a scar. "Saw it in a shop in Runcorn," he said.

My eyes began to water. My hand began to shake. What chance of me holding a tube of glue?

"We'll do it together – at the weekend, eh?"

"I don't want it," I said. "I don't want your stupid plane." I wanted to push it right off the sofa, to see how far it could fly in bits. But I turned the whole box face down instead. And maybe, in Dad terms, that was worse.

He had options, then. There were rules to this game. He could have clipped my ear and sent me to bed, back to my banana-shaped single mattress. He could have said how bloody ungrateful I was. He could have lectured me about 'the situation'.

He could have just taken the box away.

Instead, he sank down and talked to me through the back of the sofa. "I'm just trying to do what's right," he said, in words broken up by fabric and sobs. "I'm just – trying – to do – what's – right."

Ginger got restless. I did too. I ran from the room and the dog came after me.

I ran into the fields at the back of the house until my foot hit a stone and I tumbled to the ground and the uncut wild grass came up and swallowed me.

Ginger barked and barked and barked.

And I wanted him to stop, because I couldn't hear my voice. And that meant *she* couldn't hear me either.

Wherever she was, I *wanted* her to hear me.

I wanted her back.

I wanted my mother.

FOUR

At Chevington High School, they gave me tests. They tried to find out what I could and couldn't do. They put words in front of me: acne, periscope, mutual, charisma. The headmaster said to me, "Can you spell 'necessary'?" I could, but not the way he wanted me to. He had horn-rimmed glasses and a murderer's stare, a bow tie anyone would want to twang. He asked me what the capital of Turkey was.

I was 'promising', he said, but technically-minded, suited to one of the practical streams. He didn't rule out the chances of improvement. Kids like me could go one of two ways. If I was stable and I buckled down, maybe I'd step up a class or two. He patted my shoulder, shook my hand.

By the end of that year, I'd won eight prizes.

They moved me up the ladder. Began to take note.

They pushed me harder, even though I was damaged. At parents' night my grandmother talked about Prestonne. The headmaster tapped his ink-stained thumbs. There were scholarships, he said. Very few pupils from Chevington passed.

In the playground I was a nobody, a ghost. The tall skinny kid who lived with corpses and looked like one of them for most of the time. A rumour went round that I slept in a coffin, talked to bats, ate spiders for breakfast. But that was as bad as the ribbing ever got. I had a neat left foot. I was good in the air. That year, the team won football medals, thanks to my goals from free kicks and corners. Soccer was the glue that bound us together. It didn't matter to the Chevington crew that I was smart.

At Nana's, everything was quiet for a time. Once I'd settled in to the daily walk to school they left me to Ginger and the wasteland and the grass. I was the anonymous member of the house. A mouth to be fed. A pet to be patted. I occupied corners, commanded the stairs, appeared in silhouette when lightning struck. I listened behind doors when Dad and Grandad argued. I floated in their ether, dissolved behind their eyes. I didn't ask questions.

But I took it all in.

My father was struggling to cope with his loss. My mother, she was a complicated call. So my sisters became his growing obsession. He would take me out on Sundays, in Alice, the Zephyr. No ice creams, no zoos, no theme parks, no sand. We always took the same stretch of roadway, east, and we always ended up at the same destination, crawling round narrow cobbled streets or sitting in the rain among a row of parked cars. On the third trip, he finally confessed his motive. He nodded at a nondescript terraced house and said, "That's where they are. That's where they're hiding. With your other nana. Your mum and the girls."

I recognised it then. We'd been here before. When I was younger.

When we were happy.

"Are we going in?"

Dad rested his elbow on the lip of his window, nervously chewing at the edge of his thumb. He looked sideways at the house for the longest time. "We're not welcome," he said.

"Then why are we here?"

That crippled him deep inside. He rested the butts of his palms on his eyes. Like a drowning man trying to recover his breath, he sat up, straightening his body – and his mind.

"Go and knock," he said.

I looked at the house. Silent. Moody. Flowers growing limp in a window box.

"If *I* go, there might be trouble," he said. He pulled a black curl across his forehead, took the key from Alice's ignition. "Just tell your mum we're here and we'd like to see the girls."

"But—?"

"Tell her I want to talk, that's all."

"But—?"

"Go on, it'll be all right." He leaned across my lap and opened my door.

"But what if *Philip*'s there?"

My father turned rigid, his gaze ice cold. "He won't be. His car's not around. Now go."

So I walked across the road and I knocked on the door. I hadn't seen my mother for several weeks. And I wasn't about to see her now. In the bay, to my right, the voile curtain was suddenly swept aside. My grandmother's raw-boned face peered out. She looked like a Punch and Judy doll. Before I could raise my hand to wave, she had crossed to the opposite side of the bay. I heard her screech 'Bill!', my grandfather's name. He was next to appear at the window.

His was the kindest face I knew. Gentle. Round. Eyes as sad as a giant panda's. He touched his elderly hand to the glass. From his fingers ran five longs rays of despair. "Oh, heck," I thought I heard him say. My grandmother snapped the curtain shut.

Suddenly, Dad was right behind me, thumping the door with the side of his fist. He called Gran's name. "Ada, open up!"

"Neville, you've been told not to come here!" she said.

"I want to see Marlene!"

"Marlene's not here. And we wouldn't let you in if she was, you know that."

"I want to see my girls! I've a right to see my children!"

"Go away, Neville, or I'm phoning the police."

"Neville…" My grandfather's voice was calm.

"Bill?" Dad pressed his face to the door. His fingertips tested the thickness of the wood, like a bank robber listening for a combination. "Bill, let me in. Let me see her."

"You heard it from Ada. She's not here, lad. Now, what's shouting going to solve, eh?"

Further down the hall my grandmother said, "I'm phoning. He's been told. I'm phoning. I am."

"Bill, I just want to talk," Dad said.

There was silence behind the door.

Dad stood away. Hurt. Frustrated. As if he'd been turned from the gates of heaven. "Marlene?" he yelled at the upstairs windows. I thought he'd throw gravel. Make semaphore waves. Instead, he pummelled the door again.

Two houses along, a neighbour appeared. "What the bloody hell's going on?" she said.

"Mind your own sodding business," said Dad. He grabbed my arm and hauled me down the street.

"Where are we going?"

"Round the back."

The houses were locked together in fours, with a short side entry to a common passage that tradesmen and bin men and kids with dirty feet all used. My dad found the gate to my grandparents' house. With one stiff charge he knocked it clear of its retaining bolt. He went to the back door and rattled the handle. A cat on the outhouse roof next door picked itself up and scuttled away. I stood in the yard and looked into the house. The back room, like my grandparents, was surviving on a pension. A fireplace. Chairs. An old dining table. A standard lamp. Telly. A steam engine print. One degree posher than a council estate. Too small, surely, for a family of five.

My grandma appeared at the window, raging. "Get off my bloody property, you animal! I'll have you banged up for this, I will!"

And then my father got his chance. The back door opened and my grandad took control of his castle. He came down onto the middle step of three. An agent of peace in braces, slippers and a collarless shirt. He glanced at me briefly, grey pity sucking the air from his cheeks. "Neville, what's this about?" he said. I'd never heard my grandad raise his voice. His wife could grate a block of cheese with hers. It made me wonder how they'd ever got together.

"Bill." My dad took a quick pace forward.

"Neville, no," he said, raising the hand that would normally be carrying a glass of stout ale. "I can't let you come any further, lad. If you step into this house, it'll count as trespass. The boys in blue are already on their way. If you leave now, quietly, I'll smooth the waters. I'll see to it they've had a wasted journey. You won't solve anything by acting up. Please, Neville. Think of the boy."

"Just answer me one thing," Dad said, panting. "Is Marlene in there or not?"

My grandad looked away down the alley. His big toe poked through a hole in his slippers. It gave a slight upward twitch. There was no way of telling if it meant anything.

But Dad was only ever going to see it one way. "Sorry, Bill," he said, and barged right in. My grandad, with the wisdom of an Indian chief, passively accepted what was to be. He looked at me and held out a mantling arm. Together, we followed Dad into the house.

Grandma Ada was squawking like a startled crow. Dad stormed past her and up the stairs.

He checked the bedrooms: nothing. The bathroom: nothing. The parlour. The kitchen. The cupboard beneath the stairs.

No sign of my mother in any of them.

Police! Open up! Out front, another fist rapped the door.

"Get out," my grandmother hissed.

Dad glared at her. My grandfather ruffled my hair. He put his warm hand in the small of my back and pushed me, gently, back to my father.

"I won't stop," Dad said, heading back towards the yard. "One of these times, they'll be here. They will."

I looked at my grandad and him at me. He gestured

to the kitchen door, advising me to run. I nodded and started to quickly back away. As I went, he stepped towards the dining table.

Sticking out from underneath it was a bare pink foot.

FIVE

As early as day three, Thorpe began to notice me looking around.

We were in the library, getting me registered, when a group of senior boys swept in. One of them had hair like Frankie Lennox.

The librarian, Mr Leveret, said, "Well, this has to be a first for me, Thorpe."

"Sir?" Thorpe said, as perky as a meerkat.

Mr Leveret pushed my form across his desk. "As far as I recall, I've never taken down the details of an imaginary friend before."

Thorpe realised, then, that he was standing at the issue desk alone. He looked around and saw me cowering in the shadows, somewhere between Greek Mythology and Verse.

"Are you all right?" he asked.

The senior boys had gathered at the far end of the room. In the peephole between the books and the shelves I saw that the one with fair hair wasn't Frankie.

Thorpe crooked his knees and spied the boys too. "Sixth form. Do you know them?"

I shook my head. But now I'd have to tell him why I'd tried to hide.

We found a quiet place. A confessional underneath the kitchen windows. In the steam and the scent of suet pudding he learned the truth about me and Frankie Lennox.

"Knife?" he said. "Cripes. But that's...jolly serious. Why wasn't he suspended? He should have been suspended. In the old days, he'd have faced the firing squad for that." He shouldered an invisible rifle, *kerchow*, then kicked at the crumbling limestone mortar. "Mr Gifford must have given him a second chance. He must have kept it quiet. Probably thought it best. The good news is he won't touch you, of course. Lennox, I mean. He *must* be on a warning. A standing count. If he tried to get you now, even out of school, he'd be..."

"Shot?" I said, hopefully.

"As good as," said Thorpe. "His father would be pulling the trigger, don't you think?"

He had a point there. Without a scholarship, Prestonne wasn't cheap.

"We should find him," Thorpe said, adding rather swiftly, "before he finds you. We should go and check him out."

"No way," I said. I spat away the matchstick I'd been chewing to a pulp.

"But the sooner you face him, the easier it will be. Somewhere open, of course, but definitely not the quad." He clicked his fingers, hopping like a sparrow. "I know, the upper playing fields. Tomorrow afternoon it's the senior trials. He must be up for them. Do you know what house he's in?"

"The one that Jack built?"

"Jack? Oh, I see." He stuttered with laughter. "That's rather good."

"Trials?" I said. I began to walk away.

"Rugger. It's expected of the senior boys. We could watch. Jeffers will be there as well."

"No."

"Yes. He can't hurt you, can he?"

"What good's it going to do to see Frankie up close?"

Thorpe stroked his chin while he thought about this. "You can tell a lot of things from a glance," he said.

*

I told Thorpe I couldn't face the rugby trials. I couldn't bear to watch Frankie throwing his weight, legitimately beating up the other kids. All for possession of an oval-shaped ball. But Thorpe, never to be fazed, had a plan. Late afternoon, after lessons, before prep, he made me sit on the west wing steps. Two kids, we were, swapping football cards. It was innocent, he said. Normal activity. None of the prefects would bother us for it. From the steps, we could watch the seniors returning.

It was growing cold by the time we heard the distant clack of studs – the marching soundtrack that welcomed all the boys back down the school drive, home from their fields of mud and sweat. The first to arrive were the red and black quarters of Tudor House. Then the full yellow shirt with white collars, of Stuart. Another two minutes went by before we saw the green and white hoops of Latimer.

I put my stack of cards face down on the step.

Mr Gifford, dressed in a navy blue tracksuit, was with the Latimer sixteen. I watched him shepherding the team back in. He took position on the edge of a grassy verge and clapped the boys on towards the changing rooms. As they passed he'd lay a hand on a tired shoulder. Scuffle up some hair. Give a praiseworthy pat to the seat of someone's shorts.

The only one he didn't touch was Frankie Lennox.

Suddenly I saw him, trailing in with Jeffers. There was dirt on his knees, victory in his eyes, the sweat of satisfaction in the way he wiped his mouth.

"Look at us. Look this way," hissed Thorpe.

But Frankie, the champion of cool, never faltered. He looked at no one, just the way ahead.

As they drew closer, Mr Gifford stepped towards him. "Well done, Lennox. Try in each half. Super game. Super. Good to see last year's zeal is still apparent." He raised a hand towards Frankie's shoulder, but Frankie burned him off with a wild-eyed glare. Mr Gifford's hand remained suspended in space, then fell slowly to the whistle round his neck. He toyed with it, letting it bounce against his chest. Then he turned and followed Frankie and the team up the drive. Dropping in behind. Like a loser.

Like a lamb.

SIX

So half a term drifts by and this is how it is: I see Frankie. He sees me. Mainly in the quad. Or at prayers in the hall. Once, lounging over the upper school balcony, maybe trying to sneak himself a crafty fag. He doesn't speak to me. Or stalk me. Or throw me a glance. He never steps into my arc of fear. Thorpe, my agent, my private eyes, my *dick* (his joke, and latterly my nickname for him) closes his book. No case to answer. The bully hasn't broken Uncle Billy's harsh parole. The dimple in the chin, the chilling eyes, the gravel. It all begins to sink into the cracks in the pavement. One by one, the finely-razored hairs on the back of my neck, so long the compass of my schoolboy terror, forget to stand up at the thought of Frankie Lennox.

But all this changes one autumn afternoon, when my turn comes up with Daniel Mulhearn.

Mulhearn is a thug. A young pretender. The self-proclaimed 'cock' of the second year boys. His father is a surgeon, name in the papers. The son wants for nothing.

He likes to take it all.

Mulhearn has a swagger. A following. A crew. Physically, he wouldn't be a comic book hero. He's shorter than me, wider in the neck. A little extra space between the ears, perhaps. Handsome in a dark-haired, energetic way. Good at soccer.

But not as good as me.

This is where it starts: at soccer, on the field. Latimer versus Windsor. Green v blue. A meaningless match. A nothing win game. But it throws up a silly second-half incident that should have just stayed out there, on the pitch.

It begins with a stroke of footballing luck, the kind of break a forward can expect sometimes. Towards the end, as we're heading for a soulless draw, Mulhearn, Windsor's last man, their centre back, their captain, makes a clumsy challenge – on me. The ball, if I'm truthful (and I tell him this later), deflects off my instep when Leeman, from midfield, overhits his pass. Mulhearn, too keen to win the tackle, finds himself off balance, slightly wrong-footed. The nutmeg I play through his legs is not intentional. But it looks that way to the rest of my team. A great roar goes up as I slip Mulhearn. I'm behind the back four with just the keeper to beat. The keeper, Tennyson, is useful at maths, but he doesn't know his angles between the posts. As he comes to close me down he leaves me a gap. A five-year-old in flippers couldn't miss the target. One side-footed effort is all it needs. One bobbling pass into the corner of the net. I really don't have to try anything flash. A shot that struggles over the divots will do, that takes a lucky bounce, or clips the inside of a post.

None of that would have hurt Mulhearn.

But perhaps it's the roars of encouragement behind me or the fact that the ball sits up off the turf or that the Lord God moves the air around my feet in His most mysterious *Goal of the Month* way that makes me strike the ball with clinical venom. There seems to be no flight path, no pressure on my laces. The space occupied by eighteen yards steals half a second out of my life. I'm snapped alive again by the crunch of the rigging. The keeper drops his shoulders, his eyelids, his gloves. I turn, arms raised, to a raft of cheers.

And Daniel Mulhearn's furious glare.

It was the way I looked at him that did it, he said. The smile. The 'supercilious' grin. The chewing, even though we're not allowed gum. The finger, ticking like a metronome arm. The slightly scornful sideways spit. The brushing of shoulders as we walked back for the kick-off. I was taking the piss. Calling him on. Making him look like a monkey, he said.

So he's waiting for me outside the changing rooms. Him, Neil Olsen and Euan Barrett. He has his hands in his pockets, splaying them wide. On the home team, I have Thorpe and Leeman. All of us can see Mulhearn is looking for trouble.

As we swerve to avoid him, he steps in front of us, trying to manoeuvre me away from the herd.

"What are you doing?" I say.

"Defending," he says. He shadows my movements – just like Frankie did once. "Come on, get past me. Goal's back there." He pokes a thumb behind him towards the school car park. "Should be easier without the ball. You can try and sneak through my legs if you like?" He rickets them, making Olsen laugh.

"Look, it was just a fluke, okay?"

"All just part of the game, Mulhearn."

"Shut it, geek," Euan Barrett says to Thorpe.

Leeman swings his bag to his opposite shoulder. "Mulhearn, don't be dim. There are going to be prefects." He pans his gaze around. We've already caught the eye of a cluster of boys. Nothing draws a crowd like the promise of a fight.

"Come on," Mulhearn says. His fingers beckon. "Get past me and I'll let you go."

Stupidly, I try it. A shoulder feint. A burst. But he's quicker on tarmac than he is on mud. I think I'll be lucky and escape with a trip or an elbow in the ribs or a dead-legged thigh, but he's fast enough to make sure I bounce right off him.

"Aw! Now, that's not nice," he says, standing off and spreading his hands out wide. He looks at Olsen. "See that, ref?"

"I saw it," says Olsen. "Direct provocation. Couldn't blame you for wanting to retaliate, Mulhearn."

"Hear that?" Mulhearn says, poking my chest. He turns to his nominated 'referee' again. "What about the chewing and the spitting – and the grin? I definitely saw him *grin*. Didn't you?" He thumps me hard with the heel of his palm.

"I saw him raise a cocky finger," says Barrett.

"Ungentlemanly conduct, all of it," says Olsen. "Definitely needs to be punished, I'd say."

"Mulhearn, leave him alone," says Thorpe. "Or we'll all be up in front of Mr Perry."

"All of us? You reckon?" Mulhearn likes this.

Olsen and Barrett throw Leeman a glance.

Leeman's worked it out. It's going to be a ruck. It's going to get rough. He doesn't want to fight but there's a principle at stake. He lets his bag slip off his shoulder.

"All right, now we're talking," Mulhearn says. He undoes his blazer and drops it to the ground. "Gunfight at the O.K. Corral it is."

But it never comes to that.

We never even load.

From within the growing circle of onlooking boys, a stocky, blond-haired figure steps forward. A gold-ringed finger taps Mulhearn's shoulder.

Frankie hits him hard, just as he turns. One good punch with gravel in the palm. Mulhearn drops down, blood flowing from his nose. He won't be getting up for any kind of count.

Frankie says to Olsen, "You leave this boy alone." He aims a harsh finger sideways at me.

And that's it. Done. All over in a punch. Frankie glares at the crowd and they quickly melt away. He pulls the sleeves straight on his crisp black jacket, runs a hand back through his curled blond hair. He nods at me as if some favour is returned. I can only stay silent as he turns and walks away. Words would be meaningless.

Now, we have a bond.

SEVEN

It's as if the composition of the air has changed. Oxygen: 21%. Nitrogen: 78%. Other gaseous compounds — including carbon dioxide and the murmurs of the incident outside the changing rooms at Prestonne: 1%.

The whole school breathes it in.

Overnight, I'm a legend in the bicycle sheds. Boys who never looked at me, look at me now. My year group whisper like a field of corn. That's him. The new kid. Blessed. *Protected*.

Mulhearn becomes a caricature on toilet walls.

And Thorpe reopens his file on Frankie.

Why? he wants to know. Why would Frankie do that? Why would he defend me? It's just so…weird.

These same questions I try to put to Graeme on the night before he moves out to Wendlemoor with Gina.

"How the bloody hell should I know?" he says.

Lately, he's become disinterested, cold. He buckles a strap around his bulging possessions. Everything, apart from his assortment of soldiers, he can fit into an old green canvas suitcase. "Maybe he respects you for having a go. Maybe Larry warned him he had to repent or he wouldn't slide through the gates of heaven. Perhaps he just likes to stir up trouble." He swings the battered suitcase off his bed, skims it across the floor towards the door. Comb in hand, he turns to the mirror.

"Thorpe's got a theory."

"Who the hell is Thorpe?"

"My friend. You *know*. I told you about him. He's scared that Frankie might ask me for money."

This makes Graeme pause for a moment. His callous gaze picks me up in the mirror. "Money?"

"To protect me – from other bullies like Mulhearn."

As if the ghost of Christmas past has come knocking, something moves behind Graeme's eyes. I see him drift away to a darker place, through the cold looking glass of heartlessness, into his narrow-eyed wonderland of malice. He starts to comb his hair again in slow precise strokes, as if he might be ordering his thoughts into a parting. A hair on one of his eyebrows offends him. He plucks it out, tortures it and flicks it away. "Sounds like a talented boy, Mr Lennox. Better save your pocket money – just in case."

"I'll tell Nana if he tries anything."

Graeme responds with a scornful snort. He takes a jacket from the wardrobe. Corduroy. Brown. Worn leather patches on both the elbows.

"All right, then, I'll tell Mr Gifford."

"Yeah, now there's a thing." Graeme thinks for a moment then slams the wardrobe door. The naked hangers rattle. A flake or two of plaster falls from the ceiling.

"What?" I ask him. "I don't understand. Do you know something about Mr Gifford?"

"You know what your problem is?" says Graeme. He picks up my Messerschmitt and darts it towards me. I catch it as it nosedives into my lap. "You ask too many stupid questions." He nods at the bed he's leaving unmade. "Tell Billy there's a broken spring near the middle." And with that he picks up his suitcase and leaves.

The next day at Prestonne, everything is wrong. The ceilings seem lower, the brickwork oppressive. The thud from the boards is moody and dull. Everywhere I go, boys look at me and stare. It feels like I'm on a 'wanted' poster.

And no matter where I look, I can't find Thorpe or Christopher Leeman. Word is, they were ordered away. Taken at first bell. Collared by Jeffers. The mood in my form room is muted, edgy. There's a gentle rattle in the bottom of the inkwells, a growing cloud of pothering chalk. All around us we're sensing the ultimate danger: masters, putting their ears to the ground, touching a finger to the dust of a rumour spreading through the corridors of lower school, tasting it on the tips of their tongues. Something has muddied the Prestonne waters.

And Mr Perry does not like dirt.

It's Mr Tavistock who gives me up to the Romans. A hand on my shoulder as he comes to take the register. The condemnation is heavy on his palm, the censure clear in his monotone command. "Mr Perry," he says. "Without deviation. You'll take a mark and detention for any lessons or part of lessons that you miss. Go."

That's it. Dispatched. Dead boy, walking. Down the empty corridors. Along the boards of shame. Too confused to puzzle out what I'm going to say. Too frightened, perhaps, to say anything at all.

Then there comes a twist I hadn't been expecting.

On the turn just before the lower school staff room, I'm stirred by the sound of footsteps and a voice. Jeffers. At pace. Escorting prisoners. I dive into a short dark passageway heaped with racks of PE junk.

Jeffers, marching past with purpose, says, "If either of you turds identified Lennox your lives will not be worth living. Got it?"

I hear Leeman say, "I didn't know him, how could I?"

Jeffers gives him a slap for his cheek. "And you?" he says to a blubbing Thorpe.

Thorpe's answer is lost as they turn the corner – but I do hear something else. At the end of the passage is a gentlemen's toilet. Two voices. Heated. Arguing loudly.

Mr Gifford and Frankie Lennox.

Mr Gifford, blood vessels bursting, says, "How could you be so *stupid*, boy?"

Frankie says, "Don't you threaten me, Larry."

"Don't be impertinent," Gifford snaps back. "Remember where you are. School is still school. No matter what…foetid part we find ourselves in."

"Yeah, that might take some explaining, *sir*. What the bally hell are you doing in the staff facilities, Lennox? Oh, sorry, headmaster. I was dragged in by my history tutor for a little bit of personal interrogation. I hear he's pretty good at that. Particularly with the lower school boys."

A fist thumps hard on a cubicle door. "For God's sake, Francis. Don't you understand the gravity of this? Mr Perry is *not* a simpleton. This fracas by the changing rooms could bring everything into the open. If one of them should drop the slightest hint that you were ever involved in an act of extreme intimidation – on the street – he will be merciless in his cleansing. What on earth were you *thinking* of, getting involved with this boy again?"

A pause. My heart shuts down for a moment.

"It amused me," says Frankie, though he doesn't sound truthful.

Mr Gifford, however, accepts it at face. "It *amused* you?" He repeats the phrase again. "You won't be laughing if the truth comes out."

I hear the rip of a paper towel. Any moment now, they're going to leave.

Frankie speaks again to him, low and dangerous. "Well, if I go down, sir, so do you. So perhaps you could put in a word for me, eh?"

"Don't play games with me." Mr Gifford is deadly serious now. I hear a squeak of footwear as he wheels away. "Whatever facile spell you thought you'd woven disappeared that morning on Berry Road. I went to extraordinary lengths to cover up the incident with the knife. I could have buried you and brought great shame on your family. You ought to be grateful I kept you in school and—"

"What, sir? Wiped the slate clean? Is that it?"

Mr Gifford is silent for a moment. I can hear the air whistle through his teeth as he says, "I did what I did to offer you a solid chance of redemption. All right, I had my own...salvation at heart as well. But there's a principle here. Honour is at stake. Doesn't that badge on your blazer mean anything to you?"

"No," says Frankie. He's not laughing, but I sense the taunts in his eyes.

"This has to end," says Gifford, loud and firm. "Right here. Right now. This *can't* go on."

"Yeah, it can," says Frankie. "For as long as I want it to. You're a bad man, Larry. And bad men have to pay."

Two footsteps. The toilet door crashes open. It closes on a slow remedial spring. Frankie swings past, but he doesn't see me hiding. I'm hunched up and shadowed by a tall metal closet. But I can see Mr Gifford clearly for a second. I can read the despair in his sagging body. His mouth is set. His tie is loose. I see him slap a fist against the towel dispenser. I'm guessing he wishes it was Frankie's head. As he turns and leaves there's a hint of desperation in the quickness of his stride.

And a tear glinting in the corner of his eye.

EIGHT

By the time I've reached Mr Perry's office, Mr Gifford
has composed himself again. Silent and stern, he waves
me in.

"About time," says Mr Perry, in a voice as thick as
cooling lava. He flicks a quick glance at his gold pocket
watch, then beckons me silently towards his desk. He
points to a worn spot on the carpet where many a boy
must have stood before. Standing right next to me is
Frankie Lennox. Upright. Chin raised. Like a soldier.
Graeme, if he was here, would be proud.

Mr Gifford closes the door. He stands, like a guard,
by the old fireplace.

"I am not going to beat about the bush," says Mr
Perry. He sounds irritated that he's had to use words of
more than one syllable. His vampiric gaze comes down
upon me. "You know why you are here. Do not

underestimate the severity of the consequences if I believe you are withholding the truth from me at any point during this dialogue. I have spoken to Mulhearn. I know what took place outside the lower school changing rooms. There was a rumpus. Mr Lennox, here, took it upon himself to determine the outcome. He admits that physical abuse was administered. I— *Look at me, boy, when I'm talking to you!*"

"Yes, sir." My head comes up with a jerk.

Mr Perry leans forward, supporting himself on a tripod of fingers. There are grease marks spotting his blotting pad. "I have, over the past half hour, gathered in all the material facts about this squalid little episode. I have had the entire *script* from your companions. I know about the taunts from Mulhearn, and Lennox's unwarranted reaction to them. What I fail to understand is his motivation. Lennox claims he saw an injustice being done and merely acted to right it. Would you say that was a fair assessment?"

"Sir."

"Don't mumble, boy."

"Yes, sir. Sorry."

He rears back, tucking his thumbs into his waistband. "So you are grateful to him?"

Trying not to look sideways, I nod.

Mr Perry's lean face collapses inward. Behind those veteran torchlit eyes, his mind is peeling back layers of suspicion. One finger traces the blotting pad, as if he's designing an invisible gallows. My mouth is almost dry as he speaks: "Let me tell you something about the boy at your side. Mr Lennox is not a prefect, nor a role model, nor a good Samaritan. He has never done an altruistic thing in his life. He's an arrogant, brutish, self-motivated ruffian who has been in this office more often than the cleaning staff…"

Is this a joke? Am I supposed to laugh? I gulp instead. (I need the saliva.) It turns out to be the right decision.

"…and I can find no reliable reason why this blemish on the good name of Prestonne Grammar should ever consider coming to your aid. Given his dreadful disciplinary record, I would have expected him to encourage the fight or take dockets on the likely conclusion. Instead, he carries your colours into battle. Why?"

By the fireplace, I hear Mr Gifford shuffle.

"Why?"

The question rings in my ears.

"I asked you a question. Answer me, boy. Why

would this worthless thug protect you? What was in it for him?"

"I – I don't know, sir."

"Don't know or won't say? Come on, boy. Which is it? Do you and Francis Lennox have an arrangement?"

The mallet of his fist thumps down on the desk. The explosion creates a natural pause. Half a second extra to think. I could do for Frankie here. And Mr Gifford. *Nowt's what it seems at Prestonne.* Nowt. Why wasn't Frankie thrown to the wolves after the knife attack on me? What hold does he have over Lawrence Gifford? I look at Mr Perry glaring over his specs. I swear in my dreams he'd have horns at his temples. What would Graeme advise if he was sitting on my shoulder now? He'd talk about honour. He'd talk about war. He'd talk about loyalty and keeping *schtum*. "No, sir."

"No?"

"I don't know Lennox."

And there it is. Done. The lie I've been living is now complete.

Mr Perry stands back, breathing in through his nose. He looks in need of a nicotine infusion. "Wait in the corridor, both of you." He wafts a frustrated, liver-spotted hand.

And we turn together, Frankie and me, each of us careful not to look at the other.

Or at the historian, Lawrence Gifford.

On the chairs outside, we sit one apart. I know there is nothing I can say to Frankie and I'm not expecting him to speak to me. But after a sedentary minute, he does. He says, "This won't take long. They'll let you go and call me in. Don't worry, I've taken six before."

I nod to myself. I'm shaking, tearful. "Why did you do it?"

"Do what?"

"Mulhearn."

Frankie snorts. He tugs at the end of his nose. He stares for a while at the opposite wall, at row upon row of year-end photographs. The handle rattles on Mr Perry's door. Frankie pulls his sleeves straight and readies himself. Before they call him in he says one last thing. "Stay away from Gifford."

And then he's gone.

NINE

Around this time, the itching began. Nana was the first to notice it. She was pegging out washing in the garden one day and said, "Is that jumper irritating you?"

I was throwing a ball for Ginger, lost in space. In between throws, I'd been scratching my arms.

Nana put down her basket and came to stand in front of me. She pushed back my sleeves and looked at the red blotches round my elbows.

"I'm okay," I said. I was irritated, tense.

"You've been scratching for the past few days," she said. "Show me your ankles."

"What?"

"Your ankles. I want to see your ankles. Have you got bites?"

Ginger padded up and dropped the ball.

"Fleas," said Nana. She nodded at the dog.

Ginger looked up at her as if to say 'What?'.

I picked up his ball and threw it again, into the strawberry patch by mistake. Nana tutted, but the dog was no wiser. He was looking down the garden, rigid as stone. "Ginger hasn't got fleas," I said.

"All the same, I think Doctor Pevensey should look at those arms."

"I don't want to go to a doctor, Nana."

She ran her hand through my hair, maybe checking for dandruff, maybe just being a grandmother, a soul. "Are you worried because you're seeing your mother tomorrow?"

Ginger cocked his head as if I'd betrayed him.

My tiny patch of garden lawn began to shake. "She can't keep me, can she?" I missed my mother, but I didn't want to live with her.

"No," said Nana. "Not unless…"

I looked at her carefully. I didn't like pauses.

"It would have to go through the courts," she said. She pulled the sleeves of my jumper down to my wrists. "I'll iron a plain cotton shirt for you tomorrow."

It wasn't the first time I'd itched for no reason. Back when the family arguments had started my mother had screamed at me about two things. *Stop blinking!*

And STOP scratching!

It was the scratching that had got to her most of all. One day, she'd hauled me off to see Doctor Evans. It went like this:

"All day he's at it. He's worse than the cat. Go on," she said, clutching her bag to her lap, "show Doctor Evans what I'm talking about."

The doctor stood up and came around his desk. He undid the button on the cuff of my shirt and rolled back the sleeve, right over the elbow.

My mother said, "You should see the state of his bedroom carpet."

The doctor adjusted his yellow bow tie. "This hurt?" he asked, pressing my arm.

I shook my head. He pinched the flesh and I managed to wince. He twisted my arm first one way then the other.

"It's like confetti," my mother went on. "Flaky bits everywhere – can you imagine? Flaky bits of skin on a dark brown carpet. I'm changing hoover bags every other day."

"When did it start?" the doctor asked quietly. He slipped his hands over the glands in my neck.

My mother glared at me.

"Don't know," I mumbled.

"Well, *think*," said my mother.

"No matter," said the doctor. He pulled my head down and parted my hair.

"It's not nits?" my mother said. "He can't have nits? He's had them once."

The doctor made a humming sound and let me go. He retired to a basin where he washed his hands. My mother talked in signs while his back was turned. *Hair*, she was saying, *when we get home*.

"As far as I can tell," said Evans the doctor, "he's in near-perfect health; underweight for his height, but some boys are like that. He still has plenty of time to develop." He batted one hand and I did up my shirt.

My mother's mind took a worrisome leap. "Develop? You mean his glands are at fault?"

The doctor sat down. He focused on the fountain pen which lay on his desk. He rolled it back and forth beneath the weight of one finger. He looked at his prescription pad, then at my mother. "Is everything all right at home?" he said.

This is the question my mother opens up with when we sit down together in the front room in Sale. We've had sandwiches and cake with Grandad Bill and Grandma Ada, just like we would have done on any other visit.

But my mother and my sisters are on their side of the table now. I'm just a relative, on his best behaviour.

"Is everything all right at home?" she says. Except she doesn't use the phrase 'at home'. She moves those words to the side of her mouth and hides them like a well-sucked sweet behind her teeth. She substitutes 'there' instead. Is everything all right 'there'?

"I'm not happy about you living in a funeral parlour. What kind of upbringing is that for a boy? I hope they keep you well away from that side of things."

I'm listening to her but I'm toying with my shirt tails. Hearses and coffins are my 'paper round' of choice.

"I expect your grandmother's feeding you well? Probably too well, if I know her. You're full of mashed potatoes and suet, I bet. Lives her life by what's on her plate, that woman. Little wonder she's the size she is." She looks at me and straightens out a crease in her skirt. "I hear Neville's been looking around." Neville. Not 'your father'. Not my parent. Not my dad. She reads my confused expression and grunts. "No, they wouldn't tell you that, would they? He's coming off deliveries – to better himself. Pity he didn't think about it years ago."

Dad? Off deliveries? He dons the black suit now

and then to help Grandad, but the van is still parked on the road every week. "How do you know?"

"Oh, found your voice, at last? Straight to the defence of your father, I notice. I don't see you for weeks and when I do you're like a mouse – until Neville gets a mention. Sit up straight. You weren't born with a slope in your spine." She folds her arms. I make myself presentable. "He fancies he's got a career in selling. And it doesn't matter how I know. A lot goes on that you don't hear about. Mind you, that can work both ways, can't it? This school was a clever move, for instance."

Prestonne? I lift my gaze.

"Do you like it? Are you happy? Do they make you work hard? I never saw you as a grammar school boy." She turns her head and looks back into the past, the only place her misty brown eyes can travel. Whatever dreams and ambitions she had for me are gone.

Somehow, she knows we have no future.

Suddenly, she snaps right out of it and says, "For goodness' sake, what are you fiddling with?" She crosses the room and stretches my shirt – just like Frankie did once on the street. "Is this a school shirt?"

"Yes," I say tamely.

She runs one thumb along the white cotton scab.

"What's your grandmother doing sending you out in a patched-up hand-me-down like this?"

And oh, how I would love to tell her all the history of this mended hole.

"All right, stand up." She taps my shoulder. "I'm taking you into town and buying you a new one."

"I've got another," I tell her.

"Well, if it's anything like that one, you must be the laughing stock of your fancy new school. Tuck it in. It's hideous. I'm tempted to throw it in the nearest bin."

But that will never happen. For as I gather up the shirt tails and push the injured flap back under my belt, I feel a strange and far-away connection to Frankie. It happens in a blink, in the click of a finger, on the gentle peal of the mantelpiece clock. Some howling ghost. Some shift in time. Some ripple that leaves me dizzy and hollow. Something has happened, but I don't know what. And I won't find out until Monday.

In assembly.

TEN

They filled the Great Hall with systematic precision. No idle, bumbling, self-determined rows. One went where one was put. Where the master's hand guided. Shoulder to shoulder. Shoe to shoe. Like a rack of blank dominoes, waiting to fall.

"What's happening?" said Thorpe. In a whisper, of course. Even he, the great sage of the lower school, was mystified.

A prefect we didn't know, Carpenter (we learned), brought up a line of boarders behind us. "Look forward," he said as he grazed by Thorpe. Thorpe looked forward. We all did. In silence. We scrunched our toes. We ground our teeth. We obeyed the invisible tramlines of authority. I stared at the cavernous stage and its waves of red curtain, drawn across the back. Left of centre stood a lonely lectern. In the roof space above me, the oak beams seemed to be steepled in prayer.

Down the centre of the hall, conforming to the aged choreography of Noah, masters approached the stage two by two. The wooden steps bowed to their earnest tread. Mr Perry. Mr Tavistock. Mr Hevers. Mr Gifford. All of them, tight-lipped, in their gowns. The last to make the climb was Mr Bullenfield, the Head.

He was a proud man. Grey. Athletic. A strong head of hair. A chin made of steel. He wore his gown like a superhero wore his cape. It flowed off his shoulders as he swept across the stage. He went straight to the lectern and gripped it in his hands. He had no fears, no equal, no notes.

He simply had command.

"Boys. Masters. Reverend Winchcombe." He nodded at our bird-like RE teacher, sitting, hands clenched, near the front of the stage. "I have called the whole school together this morning to inform you of a tragic and, I'm sorry to say, deeply disturbing incident.

"Yesterday evening, I learned that one of our senior boys, Francis Aaron Lennox, had died in the most appalling of circumstances."

Several isolated gasps went up. One was from Thorpe. His shock wave crossed the gap between us, but all I could do was stand still and listen.

"The details," the Head said, drawing a breath, "are still…unclear." He paused a moment, releasing an invisible gravity blanket over the astonished heads of his assembly. As the word 'unclear' sank in, he stared down upon us with the wrath of Moses. "You will, no doubt, see much about this on the television and in the newspapers over the next few days. It is my solemn duty, as your headmaster, to notify you of the basic facts, which are these: the school has suffered a distressing loss and we are in strict and inescapable mourning."

Somewhere behind me, someone started to cry.

Rocking the lectern slightly off its feet, Mr Bullenfield continued. "And let me make it abundantly plain, I will not tolerate any rumouring or gossip-mongering or associated tittle-tattle about this event. Francis Lennox was a pupil of this school. No matter what the circumstances of his death, it is our responsibility, *as a school*, to honour him with all our blessings and respect. I will therefore hand you over to the Reverend Winchcombe, who will lead us now in prayer."

And there it was. Frankie, dead. It would be another twenty minutes of bluster and shuffle and the light of God before I knew how. Thorpe picked it up from a group of boys within two minutes of us leaving the hall.

They found him in a ditch near Beaufort Lane.

Face down, in the mud.

In his uniform.

Stabbed.

ELEVEN

Uncle Billy came home that very same weekend, but he didn't sleep over on the Sunday night. The first time I saw him was on that Monday, just after I'd walked in from school. He was in the kitchen with Nana and Graeme. Graeme and Uncle Billy were in their black suits. They were talking about the dead.

It was on the front page of the local paper. The afternoon edition. Big, chunky type.

Schoolboy murdered

Murdered.

Murdered.

No one at school had dared to say it.

I sank down. Uncle Billy folded the paper. He put it on a chair, well out of my reach. "You know?" he said.

I nodded. Of course. I told them about the assembly.

"Touching," said Graeme.

"Shut up, Graeme." Uncle Billy looked across the table at me. There were crumbs on their plates, yellow patches in their teeth. Cheese on toast. An afternoon treat.

"Has anyone talked to you about it?" said Billy.

"Why would they?" said Nana.

"He knew the deceased." Graeme was bloody well revelling in it. He raised a mug of tea to his mouth and smirked.

Billy loosened his tie. He rested one foot on the seat of a chair. "Well?" he said.

"Just the other boys," I told him, though most of them had shunned me, too afraid to talk. I'd gone from one kind of freak to another. The kid who was protected by Frankie Lennox, to the kid who'd had a bond with the kid who'd died.

Uncle Billy stared down at the table. He rolled a used teaspoon onto its back. "And how are you feeling?"

Weird. I felt weird. Like I was trapped inside a bubble. 'Surreal', Thorpe had called it. The whole thing was surreal. All day I'd been imagining the knife going in, remembering Frankie's words on the street.

Do you like it? Had anyone said that to him? Were they the last words he'd heard before he died?

"It's all right," said Billy. "You don't have to answer. But if anyone troubles you at school, you let us know."

"Why would they?" Nana put in again. She turned away and aimed a block of cheese at the grater.

Graeme was reading the leaves in his mug.

Uncle Billy traced a finger across his knee. "I want you to be clear about something."

I lifted my gaze to show I was listening.

"You say nothing, to no one, without our consent. That includes your teachers. Do you understand?"

Silently, I nodded.

"You look cold," he said. He wasn't wrong about that. Earlier that day, Thorpe had wanted me to see the school nurse. My skin was like an uncooked chicken, he'd said. Goosebumps and purple patches, right up my arms.

Here, in the kitchen, in Uncle Billy's presence, I was shaking again. Chicken. Chicken.

Stupidly, I looked at Graeme. I could see in his eyes what he wanted to say, *Cold, but not as cold as Frankie, eh?* But even he wasn't going to push his luck this time. "I'll garage the hearse, then I'm off," he said. He put his mug down with an audible *plonk!* and clipped my ear (gently) on his way out.

I caught up with him a few minutes later. He was standing by the garage doors, sliding them to, cursing the muck and grease on the padlock. He'd got a little smeared on the front of his coat.

"I've gotta talk to you," I said.

"Got a bus to catch, sorry." Buttoning up his coat, he strode out quickly along the forecourt, heading for the stop across Berry Road. He was at the kerbside before I could reach him.

"It's about Frankie," I said, looking over my shoulder. The doors to the house and Grandad's office were closed. The rain was making wet, grey patches on my shirt. Foolishly, I'd come out without a coat.

Graeme flipped up his collar. "You're not allowed to talk about Lennox, remember? The Lord thy Uncle Billy hast spoken." Dodging light traffic, he skipped across the road.

Almost immediately, a bus pulled up. 31. A double-decker to Wendlemoor. My shoulders sank. Shivering, I watched it take away passengers – yet it left Graeme leaning on the shelter, alone. For some reason, he hadn't got on. I still had a chance. I hurried across.

"Sod off, you're bad for my image," he muttered, a fag bobbing long and loose in his mouth. He bent his head to cup a hand around his lighter. He came up billowing smoke like a dragon.

"I need to tell you something."

"No, you don't."

"I heard Frankie arguing with Mr Gifford."

Graeme opened his mouth. He plucked a fragment of tobacco off the tip of his tongue, examined it a moment and flicked it away. He pointed down Berry Road. "See that big red thing on wheels?" Another bus was creeping past Wheeler's Garage, less than two hundred yards away. "For a small amount of money, it picks up anyone who waves at it and takes them for a ride in the country. You've got until it gets here. Then you turn into a pumpkin – with any bleedin' luck." He tipped a fine layer of ash on my shoes.

"They were in the bogs together."

Graeme looked me up and down.

I tutted. "The ones near the staff room, at Prestonne. I was outside, hiding. Frankie called Mr Gifford a bad man."

The ginger eyebrows tightened a notch. "Go on."

"I heard Frankie tell Larry he had to pay. It could go on as long as he liked, he said."

A car flashed by, spraying water from its tyres. Graeme raised the cigarette slowly to his mouth. He barely seemed to notice that his ankles were soaked.

I stepped into the shelter, out of the rain. "Do you think he did it?"

It took a few seconds for an answer to come, as if the raindrops glistening in Graeme's hair had fused an electrical circuit in his brain. "Who? Did what?"

"Do you think *Mr Gifford* killed Frankie?"

Heavier spots of rain came down. Big cow pats on the shelter roof. Graeme looked for the bus. It had pulled in and stopped and was winking to come out. He turned his cigarette vertical a moment, rubbing his instep against his calf. "Have you got a death wish or something?"

Death wish? I didn't know what to say.

"Go around spilling out stuff like that and you'll be the next one lying in a ditch." He held his cigarette under my chin until I shied away from the heat of its tip. "Lawrence Gifford couldn't knife an envelope open, let alone stick some kid in the gut. Besides, if he had – I'd know about it."

"How?"

The bus was yards away now. Graeme raised a hand. "I drink with him," he said. "Regular as clockwork. Monday nights. Hanford. Pie and a pint. If you're coming, bring your piggy bank; you're buying the first round."

The bus rumbled to a halt. Hanford Village. The Cotton Arms. Of course.

Graeme leapt onto the open platform, swinging on the pole like a fairground ride. "You listen to your uncle. You keep your mouth *shut*." He pointed a finger loaded with malice. "Stop after Beaufort Lane," he called.

He spat into the gutter as the bus pulled off.

The conductor punched him a ticket.

TWELVE

Later that day, my mother rang the house. We were watching TV, a game show, in the front, when Grandad called Dad into the hall. "Neville. It's for you."

From the start, Dad's voice was tense. "Marlene?" he said. "Yes, of course we've seen the news. No, he's fine. Why wouldn't he be all right?"

My grandmother laid her knitting in her lap. She said, "Turn the TV up a bit, love."

But I was turning my head towards the door instead. I wanted to hear what was being said.

"It's not as if it happened in the playground, Marlene..."

My grandfather walked in and closed the door behind him. He sat in his armchair. He didn't say a word. He picked up the paper and flipped it out. He glanced at the front page, but that was all. Without turning his head towards me he said, "Does your mother know about this Lennox boy?"

Willoughby stepped sideways along his perch.

I shook my head. No, not from me.

"You haven't told her what happened that time on the street?"

"No." Not even when she saw the shirt.

"Good," he said. "You'd better keep it that way. That's her on the phone to your father, bleating. If she gets a whiff of it, she'll have him back in court. Do you understand what I'm saying here?"

She'd have a good case to take me. Yes.

He opened up his paper. Inside back page. Always, he went for the obituaries first. "What have I told you about letting that dog get up on the sofa?"

I sighed and gave Ginger a nudge in the belly. He dropped to the floor and settled on the rug, next to Nana's balls of knitting wool. "Grandad?"

"Hmm?"

"Can I ask you something?"

His weary gaze travelled up and down the columns. "Haven't you got any homework to do?"

"I've done it," I said. "You saw me at the table." Why did he always tease me like this? "Grandad, is it right that one of my teachers gave Graeme a reference?"

"And why would you want to know that?" he asked. His voice was even. His gaze unmoved. He clicked his lower dentures out. I hated that.

"I think it was my history teacher, Mr Gifford."

"And what if it was?"

A piece of coal crackled freely in the grate. "Was it a *good* reference?"

Nana picked up a poker and stirred the fire. "What's this about?" she asked.

I picked two ginger hairs off my lap. "I'm just interested, that's all. Was Graeme sacked, Grandad?"

He stared sideways at me now, over his glasses. "Has someone at Prestonne been talking about him?"

I shook my head.

"Then why the sudden interest in Graeme?"

"He told me he worked there – but not why he left."

Grandad licked his finger and turned to the sport. "Well, that's none of our business, is it?" He freed a piece of corned beef from his front teeth. And I thought that was going to be the end of our talk, but then, to my surprise, he said, "It's my understanding that Graeme didn't fit in well at Prestonne."

"Probably gave them too much lip," said Nana.

Grandad hummed, but he didn't disagree. "As long as he does his job, that's all that matters here. He seems to have got himself settled with this girl. Maybe she'll make a man of him."

Dad burst in then, both hands whirling. "You won't believe this."

"If it's to do with Marlene, we will," said Nana. She calmly cast off a stitch.

Dad paced a little, stopped and gripped the sofa-back. "She wants me to take him out of school."

"What?" I said. "I can't miss school. It's—"

"Shut up," said Grandad. "And stop squirming around. Damage those cushions and you'll be washing down cars for the next two years." He looked sternly at Dad. "He's going nowhere, unless we or the school say otherwise. Marlene can go and wish upon a star."

"They're having a memorial for Frankie," I said. And for the first time since I'd heard about the stabbing, my eyes began to shine with tears.

"Bloody woman, she'll be the death of me," said Dad.

"Well, you're in the right place, then, aren't you?" said Grandad. And he shook his paper out and went back to the sport.

Ding!

And Willoughby rang his bell.

The next day, following Grandad's orders, I went to school as I always did. No flags at half mast. No doom clouds. No arm bands. It was just as if nothing had happened. Thorpe was flogging a hopeful rumour that we might close down for a day of mourning. But though talk of Frankie's death was everywhere, the school just seemed to run as normal – with one important exception. Fifth period, we turned up as usual for history and found the front desk occupied by Mr Mullen.

"Sir, where's Mr Gifford?" said Thorpe.

"Mr Gifford is indisposed," said Mullen.

"Is he ill?" we asked.

Mr Mullen replied, "That is not for me to say. What is for me to say and for you to give some serious thought to is the word 'revolution'. Russian, not French. When did it begin? *Why* did it begin? And what impact did it have on the great houses of Europe…?"

The days dragged by.

Tuesday.

Wednesday.

A rain-muddled Thursday.

One afternoon, I caught sight of Jeffers. Briefly. From a distance. Looking empty. Like a husk. Someone told me they'd seen him trailing round the quad. Just walking. Alone. Eyes hollow. Like a ghost. There were rumours, also, that Mulhearn's father had been seen 'exchanging words' across the bonnet of his sports car with a red-faced Mr Bullenfield. The next day, Mulhearn was absent from school.

And there was still no sign of Lawrence Gifford.

It wasn't until Friday night that everything changed.

I turned off Berry Road, onto the forecourt. Dragging my satchel. Dragging my thoughts. Pulling a long grey sky behind me. Alice was parked outside the chapel of rest. Graeme, in his suit, was resting back against her. I'd hardly seen him since the bus stop on Monday night. Everyone, it seemed, had gone into their holes. But there he was, long and lean, legs crossed at the ankles. White cotton socks. One hand in his pocket. Cigarette smouldering. Cufflink flashing. He was staring at the gravel. But he knew I was there.

"What's the matter?" I said. There was another black car parked right outside the office. I'd never seen it before. But that was nothing new. Clients came to see Grandad all the time.

Graeme dropped his cigarette as if he was playing Pooh Sticks off a bridge. With one twist and no shout he squeezed the life out of it. "Shit and fan," he said. "Shit and fan."

Ginger came running up. He nuzzled my hand. "Mr Gifford hasn't been at school this week. Did you see him on Monday night or not?"

Graeme turned away as the office door opened. Grandad was there, with a man in a brown double-breasted suit, serious turn-ups on the trousers. He, the man, was younger than Grandad, but no less official-looking. He was turning a trilby hat through his hands.

"This is Chief Inspector Mintoe," Grandad said. "Come inside. Now. He wants to talk to you."

THIRTEEN

We went into the office: Grandad, Inspector Mintoe and me. There was another man there, no older than Graeme. He was hovering, vaguely, at the side of the room, resting his arm on the filing cabinet.

"This is Sergeant Hynd," Inspector Mintoe said. He hitched up his trousers and sat on one of the bereavement chairs, dropping his trilby on the seat beside him. "He might take a few notes."

Hynd looked me up and down but didn't speak.

Grandad took his own chair behind the desk and made me sit at the corner, facing them. In a voice as serious as it got he said, "These gentlemen are here to ask you some questions – about this boy at school who was killed. You listen carefully to what they have to say and you answer them truthfully. Is that understood?"

"Is Dad home?" I said. There was a croak in my voice. Grandad sat back. "No, not yet."

"There's no need to be frightened," Mintoe said. He smiled like a pirate's cat. There was a certain kindness in his softly focused eyes, swamped by years of criminal suspicions. "You're not being accused of anything. We simply want to hear what you can tell us about Francis Lennox."

"Frankie," Hynd said. His eyes were the colour of Prestonne stone.

"I believe you had a fight with him once?" said Mintoe.

My eyes searched Grandad's. How would they know that?

"Just answer," said Grandad. He flicked a finger towards the inspector as if they were playing invisible Subbuteo.

"Kind of," I said.

"He attacked you, with a knife. Can you describe it for us?"

Red. Swiss Army. How could I forget?

"Have you seen that knife since – at school, perhaps?"

"No," I said.

"He didn't flash it around?"

I lifted my shoulders. Not that I knew.

"He never threatened anyone else with it?"

"I don't know," I said.

The inspector blinked. His gaze traced the fidgeting movements of my hands. The tips of my elbows were beginning to itch.

"But it's possible he might have?"

Possible, yes. But how would I know? "He's in a different year from me. I never really saw him."

Hynd opened a notepad. "You never saw him?"

"Just…you know, around," I said.

Feeble. Confused. The answer of a boy concealing a secret. Mintoe knew it. His sergeant pursued it. "But he came to your rescue once, didn't he?"

"Rescue?" said Grandad. His jaw slackened so much it almost hit the desk.

I dropped my head. He knew nothing of it. Dad and Uncle Billy, *they* knew nothing of it. Now the whole world was going to hear how me and Frankie Lennox were bonded by his fist. "I don't know why he did it," I said.

"Did what?" said Grandad, thunder in his chest. The scent of formalin rose by one part per million in the room.

Mintoe showed a hand. "Let the boy tell it. In his own time." He nodded at me to go on.

So I told them what had happened outside the lower school changing rooms. How Frankie had laid Mulhearn out flat.

Grandad pressed back into his chair. Later, to use his favourite phrase, there was going to be hell to pay.

"Tell us what happened afterwards," said Mintoe. "We know that Lennox drifted off, but did you or your friends…?"

"Thorpe and Leeman," Sergeant Hynd filled in, lifting a page of his notes with one finger.

"…Did any of you go to Mulhearn's aid?"

I shook my head. It felt as light as candy floss. This was scaring me now. Who'd *talked* to them? How much did these policemen really know? "Thorpe tried to," I said, "but…"

"What?" said Hynd.

"His friends, Mulhearn's friends, they wouldn't let him near."

"Did they fight?" Mintoe asked.

I shook my head again. There had just been a stand-off. Raised fists. Threats.

"Threats?" said Hynd.

"They said they'd get us."

"And did they?" He dipped into his jacket for a pen. *Click-clack.* Just like cocking a revolver.

The inspector brushed the back of his hand across his knee. His soft gaze narrowed by several degrees. "Did you know that Lennox broke Mulhearn's nose?"

I relived the punch. The sickening crack. Mulhearn's whimper as his knees gave way. Horrible. I felt for the edge of the desk.

"Did they come after you?" Hynd said again.

There was a pause. Two or three seconds, at most. Suddenly, my head became the axis of the planet. I looked at the cross on the wall above the desk.

"Maybe not – while Lennox was in the way?" said Mintoe.

And then I was retching from a deep dark place. Hynd, athletically, snatched up a wastepaper bin and thrust it in front of me, just in time.

"Jesus Christ in heaven," said Grandad. I'd never heard him sound so shaken. "I think that's enough," he said to the police. For once, he laid a comforting hand on my shoulder.

From the corner of my eye, I saw Inspector Mintoe pick up his trilby. He came over and slowly crouched down beside me. In a quiet voice he said, "Tell me the truth: have Mulhearn and his gang taken any kind of revenge?"

"No," I said, sick trailing off my lip.

He knuckled me, making me look at him a moment. "They won't," he said. And he stood up to leave.

But at the door, he pointed his hat at me and said, "One last thing. The knife. The one that Lennox attacked you with. Do you think it could have been confiscated? By the teacher he was made to report to, perhaps?"

"I don't know," I said weakly.

He nodded to himself. "Well, if you should by any chance hear what happened to it, you'll let us know, won't you?"

"Of course he will," said Grandad.

Mintoe nodded again. He gestured to Grandad to come outside. "A word," he said quietly, "about the other business."

Grandad followed him onto the forecourt.

They passed in front of the open office window. Their first words were lost behind the crunch of gravel, but I thought I heard Mintoe say, "Just a few days, until it's all done." And then, "We won't need to speak to him again." Then I heard the thunk of a car door closing, and the police were gone on a bow wave of tyre marks and flying stones.

Grandad came back into the office. He wafted a hand in front of his nose. "Are you done?" he said.

I offered him the bin.

He shied away, frowning. "Take it to your nana. Get it disinfected. Go on, I've got a client coming in at five." He took off his glasses and polished them with vigour on the lining of his jacket.

"Grandad, what did the police—?"

"I said, take the damn bin out!"

At that moment, the outer door clattered open and Dad walked in along with Uncle Billy.

"Jesus," Uncle Billy said, pinching his nose. "It smells worse than the bogs at the Dog and Gun in here."

Dad saw me with the bin and felt the tension in the air. "What's happened?" he said.

Grandad, calmer now, pointed to the chairs. "Sit down, both of you. We need to talk. Not you," he said to me. "You go to the kitchen and do as you've been told – then send your nana in here."

"Why? What's happened?" Dad repeated. He slipped a warm hand round the back of my neck. "Is he ill? Does he need to see a doctor?"

"He needs rest," said Grandad, his bottom lip skewing. He looked at me and flicked his head towards the door.

And this time I did leave the office, carrying my fear in yellow circles of vomit at the bottom of a metal wastepaper bin.

FOURTEEN

I went to the end of the garden with Ginger and hid myself away among the overgrown grasses. When Dad finally found me, twenty minutes later, I was slumped against the trunk of the old apple tree, splitting rotting apples with the edge of a stone.

He hunkered down and picked up a Y-shaped twig. "How are you feeling?"

"You weren't there," I said.

His face darkened. He hadn't been expecting that. "I didn't know the police were going to come. They don't make appointments when they're…" His breath fell away like an escalator stair. "Well, they just don't make appointments." He held the twig in both hands and flicked it up and down. Divining for inspiration, not water. "Listen, we've been talking. Your nana and grandad and me."

"And Uncle Billy," I said. "You forgot Uncle Billy."

"Don't get smart," he said. "This is all for your benefit." He threw the twig aside. "We're worried about you."

"It was just a bit of sick."

"Not the sick," he said. "This business with Lennox."

"His name's Frankie, Dad."

He took a three-second count and he tried again: "Why didn't you tell us what had happened at school?"

I let the apple I'd been digging in roll from my hands. Ginger sniffed at it and let it go. "You'd have started up again."

"I'm your father," he said. "It's my job to know what's happening in your life. How else am I supposed to look after you, eh?"

"You weren't *there*," I said again.

And this time he felt it. A marked wave of sadness clouded his eyes. "All right," he said quietly, squeezing my arm. "I don't blame you for holding it in, but I am concerned about the effect this boy is having on you."

"He's dead," I said.

"Not up here, he isn't." Dad tapped the side of his head. He shuffled his feet to keep his balance. After a few seconds of silence he said, "Look, we don't think it's good for you to be at Prestonne right now. We think it might be best if you went away for a few days, just until this affair blows over."

Go away? Where? "No," I said.

He sighed. "We're not going to argue about this."

"I don't want to go away. I'll miss the memorial."

He pushed an agitated hand across his mouth. "We've made our decision."

"I'm not going anywhere."

"This is not your choice to make!" he thundered. And then he drove in the final nail. "You're going to your mother's. Tomorrow. That's it."

I thought about climbing up the apple tree, staying there till the autumn had finished, slowly turning brown like the fruit and the leaves, tumbling to the ground with the rest of them. Dead.

I thought about the cellar underneath the house. Me and Ginger, hidden like a pair of *Borrowers*. Coming up at night and stealing biscuits.

I thought about knocking on Gina's door.

I thought about the thought of staying with Philip.

And then I just thought about running away.

And I thought about the truth. And nothing but the truth. Coming down hard like a judge's hammer.

Bang! With a wallop on Lawrence Gifford's head. A great white lump sprouting out of his skull with one word, 'GUILTY?', written all around it. Should I have told Inspector Mintoe what I'd heard in the toilets that day? I thought about Frankie's words about Gifford. I thought about everyone telling me to 'shut it'.

Most of all, I thought about the missing knife.

For half an hour, maybe more, I lay down next to Ginger. I lay down on my side with a dog that stank, among blades of grass that tickled my face. I didn't know what to do with myself.

From somewhere, I needed a sign.

In time, cowardice or hunger or the growing threat of rain picked me up and drew me back towards the house. On the lawn lay Ginger's tennis ball. He barked at me to throw it. I threw it. Always did. It flew towards the bedding plants by the back door, deflected off a border stone and rolled beneath the gate.

Ginger followed it as far as the gate, digging at a gap he couldn't squeeze under.

Sighing, I opened the gate for him.

On the far side of the forecourt was a long blue car. White bonnet, white tyre walls, silver trim. A woman was sitting in the passenger seat, dabbing a hand-kerchief under her eyes. A man in a business suit had just got out. Medium height, straight tie, laced shoes. Hair as neat as a *Thunderbirds* puppet. He saw me and the dog and the tennis ball, and smiled. A smile that said he had been here once, with a boy and a dog and a game of fetch. But not on a gravelled space like this.

As he walked towards the office, the outer bell rang. He listened to it, (three rings), until it stopped. "Would that be for a telephone, perhaps?" he said. He had a faint Scottish accent. Very polite.

I nodded. Yes. When Grandad's in the chapel or the coffin store, the outer bell tells him the office phone is ringing.

"You live here, I take it?"

"Yes," I said. "With my nana and grandad."

He nodded. "Would you give your grandad this?" In the peg of his fingers was a business card.

"OK," I said. I took it from him.

He smiled in thanks. A set of car keys dangled lightly from his fist. He said, "You go to Prestonne, don't you?"

I was still in my uniform, minus the blazer. "Yes," I said.

He looked at me as if I belonged to him, then. As if I was a set of dice he might roll. He pressed his lips together and nodded. "Well, you take care," he said.

"You take care."

Ginger waddled up to me, ball in his mouth. We watched the car glide through a three point turn, before it pulled out onto Berry Road. It turned right towards Prestonne, Wendlemoor and Hanford. For some reason, I wanted to wave to it. Only when it was gone did I look at the card. Financial Services. Life Assurance. Pensions. In gold italic writing at its centre was a name.

Gavin J. Lennox.

There was my sign.

I'd just been talking to Frankie's dad.

FIFTEEN

"He's coming here, isn't he?!"

I burst into the corridor, past the office, fighting with the rows of pegged up coats.

Dad was in the hallway, on the second line, putting the receiver slowly on the rest. I yanked him by the elbow and turned him towards me.

"He's coming here, isn't he?"

His face went from one kind of thoughtful to another. "Who is?"

"Frankie. We're burying him, aren't we? I just saw his *dad* outside!"

Dad looked to the ceiling, the closest thing to heaven. But a thread, once pulled, soon becomes a hole. This was the 'other business' Mintoe talked about. Now their conspiracy was out in the light.

"What the *hell* is all this noise?"

Grandad suddenly came storming from his office, looking like a half-dazed, wild west sheriff. Collarless shirt. Watch chain in the waistcoat. Rattlesnake venom in his bulging eyes.

"He knows," Dad said.

I held up the card. Grandad snatched it away from me. He didn't even need to look at the name. "This is a business," he barked in my face, the subtle sweet tang of gin was on his breath. "How am I supposed to take important calls with *you* bellowing your mouth off in the hall?"

"Dad, he knows," my father said again.

"Well, it makes no difference," my grandfather said. "He's going to his mother's and that's an end to it."

"I won't!"

Whap!

His palm scythed my ear like the crash of a cymbal. A blow that would hurt for a long, long time. Way beyond the memories of Frankie Lennox. "Don't you *dare* talk back to me," he said. And it might have been the ringing heat in my ear, but the quietness of the snarl only made the pain worse.

For once, my father rode to my rescue. No white charger, more white mouse. "I've just spoken to Ada," he said. "Marlene's away on a break – with Philip."

"More bloody lies."

"No, I don't think so." Dad's fingers caressed the curve of the phone.

And while he breathed out and Grandad breathed in, I risked the other ear and leaped at my chance. "Grandad, please. I just want to be here for Frankie's memorial. I just want to pay my last respects."

I saw his face soften. A judder at the lip. This was a language he understood. The language of grieving. The poetry of death.

He searched my eyes for any cruel ambiguity.

Finding none, he sent me to my room.

I'd been up there for about an hour when the door creaked open and Billy stepped in. "Don't look so surprised," he said. "I used to live here once, remember?"

Since he'd been back, he'd slept at home twice; other times sharing a flat with his mates. He hitched his trousers and sat down quickly on the edge of the bed, patting the mattress like a faithful friend. "How's it been with Ginger – man, I mean, not dog?"

For the first time in a week, I managed to laugh. Graeme, had he heard that, would have gone mental. But he'd never challenge Billy. Billy would kill him.

Uncle Billy has trained with the Territorial Army. "All right," I said. "He liked bossing me about. He smoked all the time – and talked a lot."

"Aye. Mainly from a small tight orifice, I bet. I hear he's shacking up with Gina Theakstone?"

"Do you know her?"

"Used to. A lot of people did."

"I like her."

"I bet you do," he said, flicking up an eyebrow. He smiled at his poster of Audrey Hepburn. "Actually, she's all right, Gina. Though God knows what she's doing with a loser like Graeme. You've met her, then?"

"He brought her here once. For tea."

For a moment, my uncle's gaze fell inwards, as if he would have liked that privilege himself. Then, in a sudden change of expression, he reached down by his feet and picked up something from the fluff on the floor. "What's this?"

It looked like a shield from one of Graeme's knights. My mind jumped back to the house in Wendlemoor. The crazy way he'd smashed the other knight to bits. The look in his eyes when he'd seen me holding Gina. How he'd never let me near her since. "Graeme makes models. He'll want that back."

"Oh, yeah," Billy said, examining the piece. "He

plays war games, doesn't he?"

"War games?"

"Mmm. All the thrills and spills of war on a table. He tried to get me interested once. He's part of some society that re-enacts battles. Safer if you do it with plastic men."

"Mr Gifford," I said on the shallowest of breaths. And just like that, their connection made sense. He and Graeme must have played war games together. A passion, shared. No wonder they were pals.

"Gifford? How do I know that name?"

"He's a teacher at Prestonne. The one you told Frankie he had to report to."

His eyes slanted upwards, retrieving the memory. "The bloke Graeme drinks with? He teaches you now?"

"History."

"That figures. Is he any good?"

I found myself nodding. "Yes. I like him. He's…" Brilliant, actually. The best teacher I ever had. Kind. Funny. Interesting in class. So why did Frankie warn me to stay away from him?

"Aye, well." Uncle Billy tossed the shield aside. "It's not Graeme and his mates that I came to talk about." He waited till he had my gaze, then said, "This burial.

You really think you can cope with it?"

He gave me a moment to think it through. "He protected me," I said. I wasn't backing out of this. I felt I owed Frankie something in return.

Uncle Billy raised his chin. Had there been a bubble sitting on his tongue it would have been absolutely still and level. He laced his fingers and twiddled his thumbs. "It's not the service everyone's worried about, you know. No one's going to stop you offering prayers to the lad. But his body is going to be embalmed. It'll sit in that chapel till we load him up on Tuesday. Are you sure you want to be around for that?"

I nodded tautly, trying not to break. "Why is he coming to us?" There were, after all, several funeral directors spread around the town.

"Apparently, we've done work for the family before."

"Do they know about me and Frankie?"

"I'm not sure," he said. But I could see him working through the implications. Mintoe and Hynd must have surely told the parents what their son liked to do with knives – but maybe not identified me as a victim?

He slapped his thighs and got to his feet. "Anyway, your grandad's given it his blessing. You can take a day from school to go to the service. Promise me, no nightmares."

"I'll be all right," I told him.

He tousled my hair and looked at me kindly. "Find something to do in the morning."

"Why? What's happening in the morning?"

"We're picking him up from the mortuary," he said.

SIXTEEN

At the top of the stairs, just outside my room, a small window looks out onto the forecourt. Ignoring Uncle Billy's advice, this is what I do the next morning: hover. I can't help it. I have to see Frankie arrive.

On the stroke of eleven, Betty rolls up. She stops without a sound, barely kissing the gravel. Grandad and Uncle Billy get out. There's rain in the air, no colour in the sky. Everything is monochrome. The undertaker's code.

They open the doors at the back of the hearse and slide a plain pine coffin onto a trolley. Grandad, looking tired and a little jaundiced, beats a phlegm-ridden cough from his chest. He peels through his keys, then unlocks the building next to the chapel, a place I've never been allowed to enter. It has no label. It has no sign. 'The lab', Graeme calls it. 'The pickling room'.

He's told me more than once what happens in there — though Grandad is sworn to secrecy about it. Frankie will be laid out and 'dressed for view'. His veins, if they haven't been drained already, will be pumped through with foul-smelling formalin. He'll be preserved, eyes closed, so the mourners can see him.

He'll be made to look pretty again before he rots.

In the house, no one talks about the body. It's paperwork. A number. Just another job. Life goes on as it always does. We eat. Move about. Watch TV. All-in wrestling on the Saturday afternoon, followed by the checking of the Football Pools. Church the next morning (for Nana at least). The roast beef and Yorkshire. The Sunday papers. The weekly bath and hair wash. Homework. Bed.

On Monday, they hold the memorial at school. It's been eight days since Frankie died. Murder, it seems, puts everything on hold. Yet no one above the age of eighteen can bring themselves to utter the term. It's not a murder, it's a grave misfortune. Not a slaying or a slaughter or an execution. It's a tragedy, a waste, a desecration of a life.

All of this passes me by in a blur.

No one, not even Adrian Thorpe, can shake me from the stupor that settles like a damp fog over me that day. All I remember on the walk up Berry Road is Thorpe telling me the story of how he was once concussed by a wet leather football and spent the entire second half of a game wandering into offside positions. That's what I am, he says, kind of offside. As we reach his bus stop, he clamps my shoulder. "You're definitely going to go?" He means to the funeral.

I can't even find the energy to nod.

"See you Wednesday, then," he says, and leaves me to it.

I gulp and wave goodbye.

That night, the rain comes down with purpose, dragging a bone-chilling coldness with it. The gutters overfill. The downpipes gush. But it doesn't stop the cars rolling onto the forecourt. Right into the middle of the evening they come: mourners, paying their penultimate respects. The chapel isn't usually open this late. But we've never had a body like Frankie before.

The last to leave are Frankie's parents. Theirs is the final umbrella to close. Mrs Lennox is a slender, frail-looking woman. Blonder than her son and intensely pretty. Hair as straight as the strings of a harp. The outdoor light is fuzzy in the rain but I can clearly see her eyes, all messed with grief. As Mr Lennox fights to open the car door for her, she covers her face and her knees give way. He drops his umbrella and catches her at once, gathering her limply against his body as if she is made from straw and rags. And there they sway, melting into one another, even though the rain is pelting down.

Grandad, there to chaperone their sorrow, picks up the brolly and endures the rain with them. When they're ready, he sees them into their car. He waits until the forecourt is completely empty before turning back to the chapel once more. Graeme, in his overcoat, is on the chapel step. He and Grandad exchange a few words, and then Grandad hurries back into the house.

Graeme, typically, lights up a fag. He stares horizontally into the rain. On his second drag, he makes an abrupt decision. He flicks the fag away and his eyes roll upward. My heart bangs wildly against my chest. I know he's seen me. He probably knew I was here all along. But he doesn't mouth abuse or show me the finger. He just keeps staring, hard and strong. Then his hand dips into his overcoat pocket, and slowly and deliberately he draws something out. I see a flash of light and I think at first he's holding up a lighter. I have to squint to see a small flame growing from his fist. A flame that doesn't flicker or stutter in the rain. It takes me a second to work out why. Then my lungs fill up and my veins grow big and I have to step away and lie flat against the wall. When I show my face at the window again, Graeme spins round and walks into the chapel.

Taking a red Swiss Army knife with him.

SEVENTEEN

"Shut the door."

I hear Graeme's voice the moment I go in. He's somewhere behind the velvet curtains that screen the small foyer from the rest of the chapel.

"And switch off the outdoor light," he says. "This is a private viewing."

I do as he says and turn to face the curtains. I'm shivering. Water is dripping off my hair.

"Come on," he says, "what are you waiting for? It's the greatest show on Earth and it's free to enter."

What I'm waiting for is Grandad's voice in my head. The only time I ever came across a dead body (in the coffin store, waiting to be moved to the chapel), my bones dissolved and my limbs turned to putty. Grandad stepped in before I could faint. He addressed the situation but he didn't ball me out. He put steel in my spine and wisdom in my heart. He showed me to the door and he told me quietly: *Go back to the house. Don't worry about this. It's only the living that can hurt you...*

Slowly, I draw the curtains aside.

The chapel is a small, sweet-smelling room. I've seen it two or three times before, but never occupied or bathed in rose-coloured light. A long rectangular table, draped in the same plush velvet as the curtains, takes up most of its narrow length. There is space to walk around, despite half a dozen chairs. In the wall is a circular stained glass window. Angels fluttering around the cross. The lion lying down with the lamb. Graeme is standing there, blotting out Jesus, looking down into the open coffin. I can just see a wave of Frankie's hair.

"He's not gonna sit up," Graeme says.

All the same, I imagine that he might. Life is not a film, my mother often says. But has she seen *Night of the Living Dead*? Filling my lungs, I take a step forward – enough to see Frankie's face. Part of Grandad's job is to make the deceased look calm and peaceful. That's the whole point of the room next door. But Frankie just looks the way he's always done. Hard. A little moody. Tight-lipped.

But dead.

Bizarrely, all I can say is this: "Why is his skin so shiny?"

"Moisturiser," Graeme says. To my horror, he rubs a thumb across Frankie's brow. As well as the smear he's produced on the skin I think I can see a line of stitches, hidden underneath the thick blond hair. "Better than a day at a health spa, is this. Have to give the old man his due: he knows how to dress a stiff up right. Bet you your chum's got more colour now than he had when they pulled him out of that ditch. Do you want to know how he was killed?"

My throat begins to burn. Is this a confession? Is he telling me, now, it was him who did it?

"Single thrust to the heart," he says. "Slightly upward intercostal blow." He makes a dagger blade out of one hand and slides it between the fingers of the other. "Someone who knew what they were doing, I reckon."

"You've got his knife," I say.

"I've got *a* knife," he says.

"Show me."

A thin smile forms on his lips, stretching his ginger moustache to the limits. "Do you wanna see where they cut him?"

Cut him? What? I don't understand.

"Autopsy. Carved him up like a goose. Probably had his organs all over the table. I'll show you." And he takes up the fabric of the v-necked gown that Frankie is wearing and makes like he's going to tear it apart.

"No!" I say and step right forward. Now I can see the plain bare feet. The toes just blueing slightly at the tips. Frankie, laid out, dressed like a choir boy. I catch Graeme's eye again. "No."

No.

He rests his hands on the edge of the coffin. "You don't get this, do you?"

"Get what?" I say. I'm shaking. Scared. Probably more scared than I've ever been before. I wipe a trail of spit from the side of my mouth.

"In about five minutes' time, I'm gonna put the lid on this box and drive in six big juicy screws. Next stop, church. Then hole in the ground. You and me are gonna be the last to see him. This is your chance to make it right, to pay whatever 'respects' you want. Some people like to kiss them. Or take a lock of hair. Or put a rose in their hands. Or a teddy at their side." He runs his gaze all along the body. "Just think what *you* could do."

"Don't you touch him," I say. "Or I'll go and get Grandad."

He hooks his little finger in a curl of Frankie's hair.

Sickened, I turn around, ready to run.

But his voice, like a cat's paw, is quickly on my tail. "And tell him what?" The question is dangerously soft, pitched so low that I won't miss the click of a blade being opened.

I turn around, feeling the sweat in my armpits. Three inches of steel are jutting out of his fist.

"I didn't make you come in here, did I?"

He did, of course, but I'd never prove it. "Is that his?"

He nicks his thumb with the blade. Then, like a conjuror folding cards, he closes it and lobs it in my direction. "You tell me."

I catch it (at the fumbled second attempt) and let it nestle in the cup of my hands. Red. Swiss Army. Second-hand. Scratched. The trademark silver cross on the shield. It's *his*. My heart pounds. "Where did you get it?"

"Open it," he says. "Be careful of the corkscrew. That's stiffer than he is. Needs a bit of extra lubrication on the pin."

I close my fist around it, feeling its bulk. I'm struggling to believe this. "Where did you *get* it?"

Five seconds go by – and then we draw.

"Won it in a game of chance," he says.

"Liar."

He laughs and fires again. "Found it washed up on Southport Sands. Bought it in a junk shop on Castleford Road. Mugged an old veteran of World War Two. What difference does it frigging well make where I got it? It's in your sticky little fingers now. The question is, what are *you* gonna do with it? Run to your grandaddy? Run to the police? Whittle a stick for your dog to fetch? You could stick it in Frankie's eye, if you like. Trust me, kiddo, he's not gonna feel it."

"You killed him," I say. And I'm backing away now, searching for support from the rose-coloured wall.

"Me? Nah. Why would I do that?"

"You're a murderer."

"No." He shakes his head. "I was with Gina, looking at prams. Oh, yeah," he says, when he sees my lip wobble. "We're having a nipper. Didn't nobody tell you?"

"You're a *liar*," I spit at him, and turn away again.

"So you don't want to hear about Larry?"

The words thud into my back like an axe. An axe attached to a short piece of rope. One tug and I'm forced to face him again. "Is that where you got it? Off Mr Gifford? Did Mr Gifford take the knife away from Frankie?"

Graeme smiles and pinches the end of his nose. He

walks across the chapel and grabs the coffin lid, holding it upright, like a surf board. "Larry had the upper hand that day," he says, wagging a finger to emphasise the point, "the day that Billy sent Lennox to report. He was smart. He knew that Lennox was scared. He told your boy straight: if he was caught in possession of a blade like that there would be nothing that anyone could do to protect him. So they did a deal, Larry took the knife and Lennox walked free. It sat in Larry's drawer until last Monday night when he met me for a drink at the Cotton Arms. By then, the cops had been to see him, wanting to know about Lennox's disciplinary record. It didn't half give Larry the willies to discover that they knew about your *drama* on the street."

"Who told them – about me and Frankie?"

"Some prefect."

"Jeffers?"

"Don't know. Doesn't matter. All the rozzers were interested in was the knife."

I let my hand loosen around it. Suddenly, it felt like a burning coal.

"That was when the panic kicked in for Lawrence. Talk about a rock and a very hard place. Should he withhold a vital piece of evidence – or show them the knife and risk losing his job."

"What? Why would he lose his job?"

Graeme laughs without any shred of compassion. He stands the coffin lid against the table edge and empties a handful of screws from a box.

Behind me, I hear the chapel doors creak. I gasp, thinking it might be Grandad. But it's only the wind playing push with the hinges, playing boo with the ends of my nerves. I can't make sense of what Graeme is saying, and my mind is all the while drifting back to the argument I heard from the staffroom corridor. Mr Gifford's angst-ridden voice: *I went to extraordinary lengths to cover up the incident with the knife...* Why would he do that? Why hush it up? Why protect Frankie at all, I want to know? And why had Frankie called him a bad man?

Graeme picks up a drill and plugs it in. The sudden buzz of its motor makes me jump. "He wasn't *protecting* him, you tosser. He was evening up the score." He laughs at my vacant expression and decides to extend me a little more line. "Larry's weak, not bad. He likes to jump into the showers with his boys after rugby. All that soap and water and flesh – it makes him go soft in the head and hard in the unmentionables. Don't ask for his sponge, if you get my drift. Lennox saw something he shouldn't one day and tried to make

Larry buy his silence. In the long run, thanks to you, it got him killed – but not by Lawrence Gifford."

"Who then?"

He lays the lid flat across the walls of the coffin, sliding it till it's at such an angle that we can still see Frankie's face and feet. "Well, right now, you're the prime suspect."

"Me?" I say, my face screwing up.

"You've got what the cops are looking for," he says. "What's more, your dabs are all over it."

I open my hand and look at the knife. The light brings up the faint curly patterns dotted all over its smooth red surface. And I feel a rush of guilt because I can't deny that I like the weight of it against my fingers. But what if this really was a murder weapon? Where would the weight fall then?

"I'll tell them it was you who gave it to me."

"And I'll deny it," Graeme says. "And so will Larry. Then you'll have to explain to the police how you got it and why you didn't say anything before."

"No," I say. My bladder feels weak.

"Then do the right thing," he says, with a growl. "Put an end to it. All of it. Right here. Now."

"How?" I think I'm going to be sick.

"Lose it," he says, with a tip of his head. "Lose the

knife where it'll never be found." His eyes draw me down to the silk-lined coffin.

And in a moment of panic, this is what I do: I look once at Frankie's motionless face, then drop the knife into the open coffin and stumble, backwards, out of the chapel.

EIGHTEEN

I couldn't sleep. I couldn't get a wink that night. Maybe
an hour or so, just before dawn. Before Dad comes in to
grip my ankle, sitting me up like a coffin zombie raking
in a great big wallop of air.

"Whoa," he says. "What have *you* been dreaming
about?"

Panting, I look across at Billy's bed. It's empty. In
shadow. My clothes strewn over it. Somewhere deep
within my fractured dreams, Frankie Lennox was there
last night, laid out like a dead knight on his tomb,
a closed fist over his bleeding heart.

"What?" says Dad. Now he's looking too. But he
doesn't see anything beyond the mess of clothes. He
walks over and daintily picks up my pants. "Your nana
says fresh on today, all right?"

This is what I learn from my father that morning:

a boy attends a funeral in clean Y-fronts.

And a uniform. I have to wear my uniform, they say. As a mark of respect. To the parents. To the school. Uncle Billy tries to find me a regular black tie. But in the end they side with the colours of Prestonne. A day out at the cemetery.

Some school trip.

As early as a quarter to nine, we're ready. When I step onto the forecourt, washed and groomed, Frankie's coffin is already loaded into Betty. There are flowers stacked against it, spelling his name. Today, he will be *Francis*. Not Frankie. Or Frank. Today he will be his parents' little boy. Graeme is sitting at the driver's wheel. He looks smart, focused, professional, solemn. He glances at me once and looks away. There's nothing of our meeting in his blank expression, no bloodshot nightmares in his steady brown eyes.

Grandad slides into the hearse beside him. Uncle Billy drives Alice. Dad, Mary Lou. I know the drill just as well as anyone by now. They'll go to Frankie's house and pick up the mourners, then drive them to the church in Hanford for the service. While everyone is getting settled up there, Dad has promised he will come back for me.

Nana pesters me to wait inside. It's not raining, but

the air is brittle with frost. The kind of weather you can cut with a knife, she says. She means nothing by it, doesn't know she's said it. But it turns my thoughts back to Frankie all the same. In my mind, I'm staring at his moisturised face, wondering how cold your body has to be before your eyes turn rigid and your toes turn blue. I shiver and imagine him drawing my heat, as if his spirit would like us to find a shared warmth. My lips part and I want to tell him I'm sorry. For what, though? For being here? For being alive? For not telling the police what happened to the knife? That thought draws a cold line down my back. But an hour from now it's not going to matter. He'll be buried under six feet of soggy brown earth. Along with the corkscrew, the scissors and the blade.

On the forecourt, the cold is niggling at Nana. But all she does is drape Billy's greatcoat around me and leave me digging my toes into the gravel.

Dad is true to his word. He keeps me waiting no more than fifteen minutes. It will take a lot less than that to reach the church. Throwing the coat into the rear of Mary Lou, I get in and we turn around and head for Hanford.

"Lot of people there," he says, driving smoothly. "You sure you're gonna be all right?"

I nod quietly. I don't want to talk.

"Plenty of Prestonne uniforms," he says. "Older boys, I think. Probably his mates." We roll to a stop at the Wendlemoor lights. Dad leans against his elbow, biting his thumb. "Tell me again, why do you think this Lennox boy protected you?"

For the umpteenth time… "Dad, I don't know. It just *happened*, okay?" And I really wish it hadn't. I so wish it hadn't. I can hear Graeme's words, ringing round the chapel walls. *In the long run, thanks to you, it got him killed*. If I'd been strong enough to deal with Mulhearn, I might not be travelling to a funeral today.

And then it hits me, right in the hollow of my chest. An idea so simple that I can't believe I haven't thought of it before. If Mulhearn was the reason Frankie was killed, then might it have been Mulhearn who killed him?

Or someone Mulhearn knew?

"Here we are," Dad says. In the time I've spent lost in motives and theories, we've covered the distance to Hanford church. It's pretty, built of a mottled grey stone. Tall, arched windows. A single tower. From the road, access to it looks tight. But as we pass beyond the sycamore trees at the entrance, the path fans out in a lightly-gravelled arc. Dad pulls up in a space reserved for the funeral cars. As we get out he says, "Do you know those men?"

He nods towards the studded black doors of the church. Uncle Billy is there, talking quietly to Mintoe and Hynd. Graeme, his work likely done for now, is a distance away with his back to them. He's looking at gravestones, hands in his pockets.

"It's the police."

"The ones who talked to you?"

"Yes."

He frowns and goes over. Hearing him coming they turn and he says, "Billy? Is everything all right?" He goes to stand shoulder to shoulder with his brother.

"Yes," Billy says, and the police say 'Thank you', and Mintoe looks me over with his thoughtful smile. He tips his hat. Two strides and he's gone. Into the church, with Hynd at his heels.

"What was all that about?" Dad asks quietly.

"Search me," Billy says, sweeping his foot back and forth across the step. He nods at me and says, "They wanted to know if I knew his teacher."

"My teacher? Do you mean Mr Gifford?"

Before Billy can respond, organ music, marmalade thick, comes wallowing out of every pore of the church. "Come on," Dad says. He pinches my elbow and draws me forward. "If you still want to do this, we'd better get in."

Through the doors, we're hit by a wall of singing. The interior is small and artificially lit. It's warm, but it still smells slightly of damp. It's at least three-quarters full. On a bier by the altar lies Frankie's coffin. The sight of it almost makes me stall. Dad drags me to an empty pew near the back, squeezing me in between him and Uncle Billy. Two pews ahead, on the opposite side, are Inspector Mintoe and Sergeant Hynd.

Dad was right about the Prestonne factor. Black blazers are dotted all around. I spy Jeffers, three or four rows from the front. I think I see Bullenfield there as well. But the man I'm really looking for is nowhere to be seen.

What has happened to Lawrence Gifford?

Dad and Uncle Billy both pick up a hymn book. They open it (anywhere) and start to hum. When it's done, we all sit heavy with our silence. The vicar, who's been standing just behind the coffin, steps forward and announces a prayer. One of those that invites the congregation to answer. As we lower our heads I bite my lip and take a sideways glance at Uncle Billy. Like Dad, he's really just going through the motions. So I figure I can ask him, "What did the police want?"

Lord, take us into Thy heart, he drones.

"Why did they want to know about Larry?"

His frown suggests this is not the right time. Even so he mouths back, "Larry?"

"Mr Gifford."

He shakes his head. Not now.

Thy grace be with us in our hour of need.

"Why did they want to know if you knew him?"

"He's gone missing," he hisses. "Now, shut up, will you?"

Missing? Mr Gifford is *missing?*

Not ill.

Not taking leave.

Not laughing and joking in the showers with his boys.

Protect us always and guide us from sin.

'Missing' is a word that people use when they're anxious to know about someone's safety.

Mr Gifford, my teacher, is *missing.*

Amen.

I look up. At the same time Hynd looks back. And maybe he notes something odd in my face because I see him nudge Mintoe, who looks back as well. I can sense the inspector is policing me, floating a suspicion, following a lead. I see question marks lodged in his slate grey eyes. He wants to know what it is I'm keeping back. But he doesn't want an answer. Not just yet. For now, his gaze returns to the front where Frankie's father is about to make a speech.

Mr Lennox takes a sheet of paper from his jacket. He unfolds it and smooths it out against the pulpit. Someone on the front row sobs into a hankie. There's an echoing creak from the organ pipes. Mr Lennox looks over the congregation. Then raising his chin in the manner of a man who's used to addressing a crowd, he says, *My son was no angel…*

Five words that suck the oxygen out of my lungs. My shudder draws a worried frown from Dad. He taps the back of my hand with his, then reaches out and puts his arm around me, squeezing my shoulder till I can't hold back and I'm sobbing freely and trying not to topple. A hot tear drips onto the cover of my hymn book. I'm aware that Sergeant Hynd is looking. And in that moment, something magical happens: Uncle Billy pulls a white rabbit out of a hat. A handkerchief. He flicks it sideways. *Here.* It's a gesture of compassion, we all know that. But there's something about that piece of cloth that takes me onto another level. It reminds me of Frankie, lying in his gown. And in a rush, I know what I have to do.

No one, Frankie's father is saying, *deserves to*

die the way that Francis did.

"We've gotta stop it," I gasp.

"What?" says Dad.

I want to speak, but my lungs are hunting for breath.

"I'll take him outside." Uncle Billy tugs my arm.

"The knife," I say to him, forcing it out.

And Billy says, "What? What are you talking about?"

I'm so full of tears his face is like polythene. "It's in the coffin," I say.

"*What?*" says Dad.

People near to us are looking round now, wondering what the disturbance is. I can sense that Mintoe is ready to pounce.

Uncle Billy is the one staying focused and calm. "Frankie's knife?"

"Yes."

"How do you know?"

"Graeme," I say. And that's it. It's done.

In a flash, Billy's pulling me into the aisle. "The police," he says to Dad. "Get the service stopped." He guides me quickly towards the doors, pushing me along at hiking pace. Behind us, there's a general turning of bodies. Mr Lennox's eulogy has come to a halt.

We step into the light, Uncle Billy and me. He looks

around, sees Graeme, and his stride lengthens.

Graeme is lazing back against Alice, coming to the end of yet another fag. He flicks the butt away as Billy approaches. "Billy?" he says. And he's still not worked out what's going to happen, until it's too late to defend himself.

Billy swings and hits him in the side of the jaw. One good punch. With gravel in the palm. It's so strong that Graeme is knocked four feet sideways. He's sliding down the bonnet, spitting a tooth, when Billy hits him in the same place again.

Graeme collapses under a wheel arch, arms and legs closing up like a spider. By then, the churchyard is alive with sound. Hynd comes sprinting past me first. He grabs Billy from behind and hauls him away. It's not easy. Uncle Billy is fit and strong. As solid as a mountain. As bleak as a moor. "You bastard," he spits at Graeme.

"That'll do," says Hynd. But Uncle Billy throws him off. Like Frankie, he won't be done till he's done. He wants to pull his jacket sleeves over his cuffs. He wants to step away from this in his own time.

Graeme's face is purple. His upper lip pulped. He scrabbles to his feet. Frightened. Perplexed. He gapes several times at the gathering mob, then at the handcuffs Mintoe is opening.

Mintoe doesn't wait. He steps forward and says, "Graeme Boezon, I'm arresting you on suspicion of the murder of Francis Lennox. You do not have to say anything, but anything you do say may be taken down and used in evidence against you."

Graeme shakes his head. "No," he says. "No." Maybe he's hoping that one of these denials will land and take seed in Mintoe's brain. But his wrists are clamped and he's quickly pulled away, toward the black police car parked next to Betty. As they open the door and start forcing him in, he wipes his moustache, smearing blood across his mouth. He makes one, and only one, definite comment. "You little shit," he says to me.

I look down. His cigarette is burning on the path.

With one twist of my heel, I snuff it right out.

NINETEEN

One of Thorpe's favourite words was 'catalysis'. He liked the shape of it, he said. The aftertaste. The *sibilance*. The feeling of power it evoked when you spoke it. He could rattle off the definition of it, too. The same way he could with 'osmosis' or 'quantum'. *Catalysis is the process by which the rate of a chemical reaction is either increased or decreased by means of a chemical substance known as a catalyst. Unlike other reagents that participate in the reaction, a catalyst is not consumed by the reaction itself.*

In the aftermath of Frankie Lennox's funeral, anyone in Nana's house could have walked him through the perfect analogy for it.

They wanted a statement. Mintoe and Hynd. Within an hour of taking Graeme into custody, they were sitting at our kitchen table talking to me. They wanted it all, from the attack on the street to my talks with Graeme and the reason I'd confessed about the hiding of the knife. They traced every crack in every pavement. It took until the early afternoon to tell it. Then they condensed it and wrote it all down. With Dad and Grandad both looking on, they read it all back to me, word for word. Then they made me put my signature on it.

They didn't blame me. Not for a single thing. All they really wanted to know was why I hadn't mentioned the argument between Mr Gifford and Frankie when they'd come that time to ask about the knife?

Hynd said, "Was it because we didn't ask about Gifford?"

I shrugged at that and Mintoe said, "No. It was loyalty – to both of them, wasn't it?"

Dad could see my eyes growing moist. "Does he have to answer this?"

And I said, "I really liked Mr Gifford, but Frankie…"

"It's all right, son," Mintoe said. He tapped my hand and stopped me there.

"Where is he?" I asked.

Mintoe looked me in the eye. "Lawrence Gifford?"

"Yes."

"We still don't know." He stood up and buttoned his jacket.

Sergeant Hynd put his notepad away.

"What will happen to Graeme?" asked Nana. She'd been in the kitchen, baking bread.

"He certainly won't be coming back here," said Grandad.

Mintoe put on his trilby hat. He pulled the tip of it down toward me. "Sleep easy. He won't be bothering you again."

"Did he do it?" I said. "Did he really kill Frankie?"

"We shouldn't be jumping to conclusions," said Nana.

And Mintoe, with an air of justice, said, "I'm not at liberty to answer that question."

"What about Billy?" Dad asked boldly. "Will he be charged with assault?"

We all looked anxiously at the policemen. Mintoe raised an eyebrow at Hynd. The young sergeant wrinkled his nose. "I wasn't close enough to hear what passed between them. For all I know, your brother was provoked."

The inspector smiled. He knuckled Dad's chest. "Tell Billy to mind his temper in future."

For three days, my grandparents kept me out of school. I did jigsaws with Nana, played games with the dog. A strange kind of muted silence descended. But we all knew a catalyst was hard at work. And though no one, certainly not Dad, ever spoke of it, we knew the reaction we were hoping to avoid. Graeme's arrest had featured on the news. And the news was never far from my mother.

Yet when the call from her came, the nature of it took us all by surprise. She spoke to Dad first. For at least half an hour. By the time he'd called me into the hall, the lights had gone out in his eyes again. "She wants to tell you herself," he said.

"Tell me what?"

He just handed me the phone and left me to it.

"Mum?" I said.

She took a deep breath, preparing herself. I wasn't fooled. I knew she'd been crying for a while. "I've something important to tell you," she said.

She heard me swallow and her voice broke up. "Me and your father are going to be divorced. I'm going to live with Philip. Do you understand?"

"Umm," I said.

"I'm taking the girls. We're moving to Norwich."

A tear rolled gently down my cheek. It got amongst

my fingers. Ran along the phone.

"Norfolk," she said, but it wasn't making sense. The pause became awkward. She gagged a little. "Please, say something."

I shook my head. I couldn't think straight. Or find any words.

"I just want to hear your voice," she said.

I looked at the empty coats on the rack. "Mum," I said simply.

And she dropped the phone.

TWENTY

Inspector Mintoe and his sergeant returned to the house just before five on Thursday afternoon. Nana put them in the kitchen and made a pot of tea. For the first time ever, Hynd sat down. When Dad and Uncle Billy came in to join us, Mintoe stopped playing with the brim of his hat and dropped it like a tea cosy over a green, unsuspecting apple. He put his closed fist into the centre of the table. When he opened it, there lay Frankie's knife.

"Jesus," said Billy. "Is this allowed? Can you do that with evidence? I thought-?"

Inspector Mintoe raised his hand. "This is not the knife that killed Francis Lennox."

We all stared at it, as if it was a kind of imposter. All of its blades were safely tucked away.

"We couldn't be sure until we had it," said Hynd.

"We needed to eliminate it from our enquiries."

"So Graeme...?" I said.

"Didn't kill him," said Mintoe. "Neither did Gifford. We're pretty sure of that."

"Have you found him?" asked Dad.

There was a momentary pause. The inspector straightened his spine against his chair. "Let's untangle the web a bit first. The whereabouts of this," he pushed the knife gently, making it spin, "hindered our progress for several days. We were fairly certain that Gifford must have had it, but proving it was another matter. You might be surprised to hear that it wasn't until our investigation began that the school knew anything of the skirmish on Berry Road. That disclosure, as I'm sure you can imagine, made a few gowns flutter along the corridors of power. Even then, Gifford found a way to cover up the truth. When the headmaster hauled him into his office wanting to know why he hadn't been informed of a serious assault, Gifford took a chance and made up a story. He admitted to the head that he'd disciplined Lennox for a bullying incident, but no mention had been made to him about a knife. He simply denied all knowledge of it."

"But why would he want to lie to you?" said Dad. "If he didn't do the murder, what was the point of him hiding the knife?"

Inspector Mintoe smiled politely. "At Prestonne, some things are worse than murder. With so few facts to go on, we couldn't press Gifford hard on his story. We simply assumed he'd contained the incident just to protect the reputation of the school. Given what we've learned about him since, we now know that he had a far greater motive for keeping quiet." He rubbed the table top with his middle finger. "We can't verify Graeme Boezon's statement without casting another shadow over the school, but we do have sufficient reasons to believe that his allegations about Gifford's…admiration for boys is true. Lennox clearly knew about this, though we've yet to uncover how he was exploiting it. The knife attack levelled the playing field. Lennox's mistake, if mistake it could be called, was to panic when challenged and give the blade up. In doing so, he handed Gifford a lifeline. From that moment on, if any improper suggestions had been made about the master, Gifford could have had the boy expelled."

"Mutually assured destruction," said Billy.

"A spiralling madness, yes."

"But everyone knew he had the knife," I said. "Even Jeffers. Did he lie too?"

"Apparently, he didn't," Hynd cut in. He reached over the table for a ginger biscuit. "In his statement,

Jeffers confirmed the attack but claimed that he never saw the knife again afterwards. He swore that Lennox told him he'd sold it."

"By then, it was a matter of pride," said Mintoe. "Lennox was too conceited to admit that the knife had been confiscated. He even bragged to Jeffers that he'd gone through his dressing-down without telling Gifford that he'd carried a weapon. In that sense, he played into the master's hands. Later, of course, he came to resent it."

"Is that why he went for Mulhearn?" said Billy. "Just to put pressure on Gifford?"

Mintoe pulled his mouth into a line. For a moment, the only sound in the room was the slow and steady tick of the clock. "Our friends in the police psychology department will probably suggest that Francis was a deeply unhappy young man who was sending out a desperate cry for help. I don't doubt there is some truth in that. But on the whole I favour the theory that he was irritated because he'd relinquished his power." He flipped his gaze towards me. "I know you have a grudging respect for the boy, and perhaps he felt the same about you, but I agree with your uncle on this. I think Lennox came to your aid primarily to stir the dirt again. His actions may not have been entirely pre-planned, but once the ripples began to spread out, I think he revelled in it. Whether that led to his death or not is still open to question. But there's an old cliché that says if you play with a wasps' nest you're going to get stung. The difference between a wasp and a blade, in this case, was a young man's life." He turned his gaze to the knife again.

It was me who broke the ensuing silence. "Can I ask you something?"

Mintoe brought his mug to his mouth and nodded.

"Why did he give the knife to Graeme?"

The two policemen exchanged a glance. Hynd rubbed his hands free of biscuit crumbs, but it was Mintoe who spoke again. "According to Boezon's statement, Gifford was in two minds what to do that night they met in the Cotton Arms. Fundamentally, Gifford is a man of principle; a decent teacher who got himself drawn into an awful mess. I believe he knew he was in too deep and was ready to come clean. But Boezon persuaded him the best course of action was to keep his mouth shut and shed the knife in Hanford canal. Boezon took it, offering to do the deed. Being the sort that he is, however, he decided to have some fun with you instead."

"Fun? Is that what you call it?" Uncle Billy, teeth gritted, leaned back against the sink.

"He'll regret it," said Hynd. "We can put him away for a decent stretch."

"But not for murder?" said Dad.

Mintoe shook his head. He spooned some extra sugar into his mug. "Perverting the course of justice. Abusing a minor. That'll do for a start. I'm sure we can rustle up some other misdemeanours."

"He hit Gina," I said.

Uncle Billy turned his head. Under his breath, he swore at the wall.

Mintoe nodded. "We'll look into that."

Dad stood behind me, gripping my shoulder. "So who did kill Lennox?"

For a moment, there was silence. Mintoe sat back, lacing his fingers. "We don't know," he said, peering out into the garden where Ginger was chewing his tennis ball to shreds. "We've followed up several lines of enquiry, but none of them have proved very fruitful so far."

"What about Howard Mulhearn?" said Billy.

"Daniel's older brother?" Hynd looked up. "You know him. From the TA, right?"

"He's a nutcase."

Mintoe smiled again. "Doesn't make him a killer," he said. He swilled a mouthful of tea around his cheeks. Graciously, he lifted the mug to Nana. She'd been sitting quietly all this time, holding my hand beneath the table.

"If you ask me," she said, "boys like him, this Frankie Lennox, they're just..." And she didn't know what to say – foolish, lost or bad to the core? "He could have got himself in trouble with anyone, couldn't he?"

The inspector wrapped his fingers around the mug. He lifted it as if he needed the exercise, then set it back down, on a coaster this time. "That really is a fine pot of tea," he said. He gestured at Hynd, who stood up and opened the door for his boss.

"What about Mr Gifford?" I said.

Inspector Mintoe dusted his trousers. He took out a handkerchief and dabbed his mouth. He pushed his chair neatly under the table.

"You've found him, haven't you?" said Dad.

I felt Nana's hand close tighter on mine.

Mintoe picked up the knife. He dropped it in his pocket and reached for his hat. But instead of putting the hat onto his head, he held it against the middle of his chest, as if he was trying to capture his heartbeat. "A man fitting Lawrence Gifford's description was found yesterday morning in a disused barn on a smallholding in Durham, close to his boyhood home. I'm afraid he was dead."

"Oh, God," said Dad.

I looked at Nana. She put her warm hand on the slope of my neck.

Uncle Billy went back to staring at the wall.

"We don't suspect foul play," said Mintoe. He nodded at us all, lastly to Nana. "Thank you for the tea. We'll see ourselves out. I shouldn't think we'll need to trouble you again."

TWENTY-ONE

My mother used to have a favourite saying: if aliens landed on the planet overnight it wouldn't stop anyone going out for milk. We'd adapt, she used to say. Life would go on.

What she didn't say was life would be harder afterwards.

For a second time, Prestonne School was in mourning. And though the bells kept ringing and lessons were taught and the quad filled up and the rugger season ran, we knew we were really just blundering around, stumbling through the shadows left behind by Lawrence Gifford.

Mr Bullenfield once again talked about loss. He cast the word out across the hall on a line and I caught it plumb in the centre of my heart. I knew about loss. I'd suffered it all summer. It had stripped away that part of me that used to be a boy and turned me into something alien and cold. I no longer cared that my mother was in Norwich. I no longer worried I'd be bullied at school. I forgot about Graeme with the turning of the leaves.

I forgot, most of all, what it meant to be innocent.

But when the final twist came, when the transformation struck, it was as fine as a delicate reversal of the wind. Like the imperceptible movements of planets, it went by mostly unnoticed at first. Everyone around me felt its effects, but all I would personally take from the change was the lasting memory of Frankie Lennox. I would seal him up like the tools and blades of his secondhand knife and drop him in my pocket for another forty years.

The catalyst, this time, proved to be my father. One night, he parked his van on Berry Road, then came into the kitchen and introduced me to my future.

"Stand up. There's someone I want you to meet."

He reached back, into the darkness of the hall.

She came forward. Her fragile hand in his.

She was the first date of several, as it would turn out. A pleasant-looking woman with lionesque hair and a lopsided smile and knee-high boots. A teacher from the local primary school. For me, it was a moment of passing confusion. For Dad, it was the start of the healing process.

Bravely, he slipped his arm around her waist. "Joyce," he said, not biting his thumb, "this is my son, Vincent."

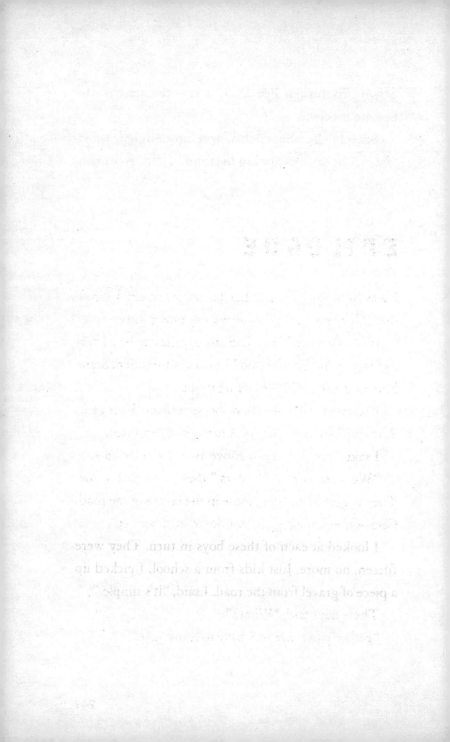

EPILOGUE

I was thinking of my father last night before I wrote this. Thinking of the way this story never ends.

It was late, and Tricia had already gone to bed. I was locking up the house when I heard a commotion. Some boys in the street, just bawling it out.

I stepped outside. There were four of them at it. Spraying lager on the cars. They'd had too much.

I said, "Hey, you boys. Move away from the cars."

"We weren't near the cars," these boys said to me. They laughed and hung loose in the centre of the road. One of them, the biggest, sat down on a bonnet.

I looked at each of these boys in turn. They were fifteen, no more. Just kids from a school. I picked up a piece of gravel from the road. I said, "It's simple."

These boys said, "What?"

"Either you move or I have to move you."

Then they didn't shake their lager any more. They could see I was serious. I had a look in my eye, gravel in my palm. Maybe they thought: this guy climbs mountains. Three of them moved as I stepped across the road. The guy on the bonnet, he slid off fast.

"I've got a knife," he said, but he was twitching, nervous.

"Leave it, Yabba," another boy said.

"Knife?" I said.

"I'll use it. I will."

I let the gravel fall from my hand. I closed my eyes, and this is what I said: "You're gonna end up in a ditch, you jerk. Just like Frankie, face down in the dirt. You'll end up in mud at the side of a road. A hole in your shirt. A good clean edge."

But I was talking to myself, to the light of the lamps.

Away down the road, some boys were running.

They were splashing lager.

Over the cars.

Questions and Answers
with Vincent Caldey

What inspired you to write *A Good Clean Edge*?

I was introduced to the work of the American author, Raymond Carver, by a friend who was trying to write short stories in a similar style. I liked the sparse, almost poetic nature of Carver's writing and decided to try it myself. *A Good Clean Edge* began as a short story but I never felt it was complete in that format. I started working on it as a novella a couple of years ago.

Is the book based on any personal experiences?

The story is loosely based on a bullying incident, in which a peculiar sort of bond developed between the two protagonists. I've always been fascinated by the mechanics of intimidation and what drives people to do it. To give the story an extra slice of tension I set it against the backdrop of my parents' acrimonious marital break-up. That element will resonate with a lot of readers, I'm sure.

How did you feel approaching the issue of youth knife crime in the book?

There are many books written about bullying. So in order to develop the main theme a little I dipped into the topic of knife crime, which was very current at the time of writing. Out of that grew a much darker, fictional element which glimpsed at several areas of abuse. Ultimately, the book was not really a comment on knife crime, but on the perils that possessing such weapons might bestow.

Why did you choose to write for young adults?

I didn't. I wrote the book as I saw it and it naturally fell into the YA arena.

Where is your favourite place to write?

I have a desk in a spare bedroom, but I can work from anywhere and often do.

When did you know that you wanted to be an author?

I applied for a job with the BBC when I left university and didn't get it. If I had, I might have been writing much earlier than this because I've always liked TV drama. I never really wanted to be an author, but like most people I've always sought a way to exorcise my demons, and writing is one of the best, if not the best, means of achieving that. It's endlessly fascinating to take on a topic and see where it leads you or what it tells you about yourself.

What advice would you give to aspiring young writers?

Read a lot. Trust your instincts. Let the story take you where it wants to go and not where you think it should go.

 Follow @vincentcaldey

Bernard Ashley

Amber is shocked when her brother falls
to his death from a tower block.

She's convinced it wasn't an accident, and so begins
her journey to discover the truth and bring some kind
of justice for Connor.

With twists, turns and a fabulous multi-layered plot,
don't miss this thrilling and absorbing novel.

'A tautly written, tough-talking teenage crime story...'
Jacqueline Wilson

ORCHARD BOOKS
www.orchardbooks.co.uk

Don't miss

Little Soldier

by Bernard Ashley

Shortlisted for the Carnegie Medal
and the Guardian Children's Fiction Award and now part of the
Imperial War Museum's Once upon a Wartime exhibition.

978 1 86039 879 7 £5.99 Pbk

When Kaninda survives a brutal attack on his village in East Africa
he joins the rebel army, where he's trained to carry weapons,
and use them.

aid workers take him to London, to a new family and a comprehensive
school. Clan and tribal conflicts are everywhere, and
n the streets it's estate versus estate, urban tribe against urban tribe.

All Kaninda wants is to get back to his own war and take revenge
on his enemies. But together with Laura Rose, the daughter of his
new family, he is drawn into a dangerous local conflict that
is spiraling out of control...

ORCHARD BOOKS
www.orchardbooks.co.uk

Shortlisted for the Carnegie Medal

978 1 84616 601 3 £5.99 PB

"You scared, Daniel?"

How many times has Tozer said that to me?
Hundreds.

But this time it's different. He hasn't got me in a
headlock, with one of his powerful fists wrenching
my arm up, asking, "You scared, Weirdo?"

No, we're here, trapped underground together...
with no way out.

ORCHARD BOOKS
www.orchardbooks.co.uk